ACROSS THE BARRICADES

ACROSS THE BARRICADES

JOAN LINGARD

HEINEMANN
NEW WINDMILLS

Heinemann Educational Books Ltd
Halley Court, Jordan Hill, Oxford OX2 8EJ
OXFORD   LONDON   EDINBURGH
MADRID   ATHENS   BOLOGNA   PARIS
MELBOURNE   SYDNEY   AUCKLAND
IBADAN   NAIROBI   HARARE   GABORONE
SINGAPORE   TOKYO   PORTSMOUTH NH (USA)

ISBN 0 435 12203 7

91 92 93 94 18 17 16 15 14 13 12 11

Produced by Mandarin Offset

Chapter One

"Sadie! Sadie Jackson!"

She looked round. For a moment she could not see who was calling her. The pavement was thick with people heading homewards. Then she saw him coming through the midst of the throng. Tall, dark, broader than she had remembered, but with the same bright spark in his eyes. She waited for him to reach her.

"Kevin," she said. "Kevin McCoy."

"It's me all right." He was grinning.

"Haven't seen you for ages. It must be nearly three years."

"Suppose it is. It's funny seeing you again after so long."

They only lived a few streets away from one another but it might as well have been a thousand miles. They stood and looked at one another and let the hurrying people push round them.

"Fancy a cup of coffee?" asked Kevin. "Have you time?"

"Don't see why not," said Sadie. There were many good reasons why not, her mother would say, but Sadie was not one to be put off by reasons, especially her mother's.

They walked side by side to a coffee bar without talking. They felt a little awkward walking together but once inside the café, seated across a table from one another, their tongues broke free again.

"How's Brede?" she asked.

"How's Tommy?" he asked at the same time, and they laughed.

"Brede's fine," he said. "She's working as a nursery nurse."

"She always was soft on kids, wasn't she? Tommy's in the yard apprenticed as a welder."

They were silent for a moment, Sadie thinking of Kevin's sister Brede and Kevin of Sadie's brother Tommy as each had been three years ago. They had all been at school then, different schools. They had started as enemies, had even fought with stones and fists; then for a while they had been friends but eventually had drifted apart because of the difficulties of meeting.

"And you, Sadie, what are you doing?"

"Me?" She shook her long fair hair back over her shoulder in a gesture that he remembered. "Well, first I went into an office"—she wrinked her nose—"and then I got a job in a linen mill..."

He laughed. "You always were a restless one!"

"Look who's talking!" They were used to sparring with one another; it came back to them easily. It was as if the three years had never been.

"I've had the same job since the day I left school," he said. "So there!"

"Is that so?"

"That's right. I'm working for Kate's da in his scrapyard. Remember Kate, Brede's friend?"

"Indeed I do. She used to fancy you, didn't she? Does she go with the job?"

"Sarky as ever, aren't you?"

She made a face at him. "I think the scrap business would suit you rightly ... roaming the streets and all that."

"The streets aren't the same as they used to be. Plenty of scrap lying about not what we're looking for."

6

Scrap in the streets: burnt-out cars and buses and armoured vehicles, torn-up paving stones, barbed-wire coiled to form barricades. And along the streets went soldiers on patrol with fingers on the triggers of their guns, men and women eyeing them watchfully, suspiciously, and bands of children playing at fighting and sometimes not just playing. Sadie and Kevin were quiet. The subject was too difficult to talk about, too difficult for them.

"It's a dead-end job anyway," said Kevin. "The scrap business. I won't stay in it."

"What'll you do?"

He shrugged. "What are you doing now? You haven't told me yet."

"I'm working in a hat department," she said in an affected voice.

"You!"

"We get a very nice class of customer." She arched one eyebrow.

"I'll bet."

"You should see some of the old bags." Sadie rolled her eyes. "Smirking at themselves in the mirror and then asking you how they look."

Kevin chuckled. "You never found it easy to tell a lie, did you?"

"You'd have to be a real phoney for this job. It is time I was looking for something else. My mother would have a fit if she heard me saying that."

"Sadie, you must have given your ma a thousand fits, I'm thinking." Then Kevin asked, "Are you hungry?"

"Starving."

He went to the counter and bought them two hamburgers each. They ate hungrily, enjoying the warm thick rolls with the meaty centres. Outside, the sun shone on the opposite side of the street. Sadie finished her last bite and sighed with contentment.

"It's a warm night," said Kevin. "It would be nice up on Cave Hill."

"It would that."

"Would you like to go up there?"

She nodded.

"Now?"

"Yes."

He guided her out of the café into the street and then dropped his hand from her arm. On the way to the bus stop they passed a newspaper billboard. SHOP GUTTED BY BOMB, TWO KILLED, ONE INJURED, it declared. They both looked away and talked instead of Tommy and Brede, remembering days spent at the seaside the summer they had all been friends.

When they reached the stop, Kevin stood with his back against the stance and looked at Sadie with a smile on his face.

"You're even better looking than I thought you'd be."

"Thanks very much!" Sadie tossed her head, but not with anger.

"At one time I thought you were going to make an all-in-wrestler. Do you remember the night you jumped on me when I slipped?"

"How could I forget it? You'd been wrecking our King Billy."

"You could run, I'll say that for you."

"Hello there, Sadie."

Sadie turned to see that a girl had stopped beside them. It was Linda Mullet, her old school friend, who lived in the same street.

"Oh hello, Linda."

Linda looked pointedly at Kevin, waiting for an introduction. Sadie looked back at Linda.

Suddenly a frown knotted Linda's eyebrows. "I've seen you before, haven't I?" she asked Kevin.

"Everyone's seen him before," said Sadie. "He's a well-known man about town."

8

"Oh you!" Linda pouted. She hated to be teased. She continued to stare at Kevin.

"He can wiggle his ears too," said Sadie.

"I've a few more tricks forby," said Kevin.

"I know who you are," cried Linda triumphantly. "Your name's Kevin and you're—" She broke off.

"Yes, he's—" said Sadie. "So now you know. I'm glad you don't have to sit all the way home on the bus with it worrying you."

Linda's round little mouth straightened into a taut line. She edged away. "I'll be seeing you, Sadie."

"No doubt."

Linda walked away swiftly.

"She can't get back quick enough to spread the good news in your street, Sadie," said Kevin.

"Let her spread what she likes."

"I always liked the devil in you." Kevin grinned. "You never let them get you down, do you?"

"Her bum wiggles just like her ma's. I could see that startin' three years ago and her tongue wags just like her mother's, too."

"I thought she used to be your best friend?"

"You're jokin'."

"Here comes our bus." The bus swished in beside them. He bowed to her. "Madam, your carriage awaits you."

"Thank you, sir."

"Come on, youse, if you're coming," called the conductor. "I haven't got all day to hang about, I'm wanting home for my tea."

Sadie and Kevin stepped aboard, both of them aware that they were embarking on something dangerous. But then neither of them had ever been inclined to shy away from danger. As long as they could remember they had always been aware of it.

Sadie bounded up the stairs in front of Kevin. Half way up she turned and looked down at him and laughed.

9

Chapter Two

Mrs. Jackson flipped the bacon over in the pan and lowered the gas so that it would not frizzle.

"Tea ready yet, Ma?" asked Tommy. "I'm starvin'." He had changed out of his overalls and washed off the grime of the shipyards. He sat at the kitchen table with his knife and fork in front of him ready to devour the food as soon as his mother would set down his plate.

"It's ready," she said. "I'm just wondering where that girl's got to. You'd think I'd nothing else to do but stand here slaving over a hot stove waiting for her convenience. It'll be a different story when it's her that's standing over a stove!"

"I can't wait to see the day," said Tommy. "But I think she's got other things in mind."

"Dear knows what she has in her mind." Mrs. Jackson shook her head and wiped her hands down the sides of her wrap-around overall. "I'll be glad when I see her settled."

"Oh, come on, Aggie, let's have our tea, for dear sake," said Mr. Jackson. "I've to be at the Lodge for seven. We can't sit here waiting on Sadie."

"You're right."

Mrs. Jackson turned off the gas. It went out with a plop. She took the plates that had been warming above the cooker and served the food, watched hungrily by the men. They began to eat at once. She poured the thick strong tea from the old brown teapot and then sat down herself. She kept on her overall. Her thin greying hair was garnished with rollers. She took her rollers out after tea to sit and watch television and when the television closed down at night she put the rollers back in again.

The men did not speak whilst they ate. They concentrated on the food, wiping their plates clean afterwards with thick hunks of bread taken from the packet on the table. Mrs. Jackson talked all the time, grumbling mostly about Sadie, shaking her head and sighing and sniffing. From time to time Mr. Jackson grunted, supposedly in agreement, but neither he nor Tommy listened. They knew what she was saying without having to listen. Mr. Jackson was thinking about the Lodge meeting. It was an Orange Lodge and they were preparing now for the big Orange Walk on the twelfth of July. He had been a member of the Lodge since his youth and his father before him, but his son was not, and the fact grieved him. Tommy was still a good Protestant, he knew that, but he did not seem to realise that you had to be constantly reaffirming your faith.

Tommy was trying to decide which film he should take Linda to see. There were two possibilities but one was rather violent and she liked what she called 'a nice picture'.

"Well, I don't know," said Mrs. Jackson. "But there's one thing, she's got no consideration for other people."

Tommy looked up. "She'd give you her last penny."

"If she had one to give." Mrs. Jackson sniffed. She got up to clear the dirty dishes. "She spends her pay the day she gets it."

"But she doesn't gripe about it."

"Pour us another cup of tea, Aggie." Mr. Jackson pushed his cup across the table. "And then I'll be off."

Mrs. Jackson poured it.

They heard the front door opening and Linda's voice calling, "Anybody in?"

Her feet tapped in the lobby and then she opened the kitchen door.

"Oh, hello, Linda," said Mrs. Jackson. "Did you get fed up waiting for Tommy?"

"I was ready early so I just thought I'd come on over." Linda sat down on the chair Mrs. Jackson had vacated and crossed her legs.

"We're a bit late the night," said Mrs. Jackson, running hot water into the sink. "We were waiting for Sadie."

"I don't think she was coming home." Linda smiled knowingly.

"Have you seen her?" asked Tommy.

"I saw her on the way home."

"Where was she?"

"At a bus stop." Linda swung her foot for a moment before she added, "She wasn't alone."

"That's nothing new. She hardly ever is." Mrs. Jackson scraped the remains of the food into the bucket. "Our Sadie knows the half of Belfast," she said, not without pride. Part of her was pleased that Sadie knew so many people, the other part resented her daughter spending so much time on them. "It's a wonder she didn't think to send a message back by you."

"I don't think she was that fussy about me seeing who she was with."

"Who was she with?" asked Mr. Jackson, taking an interest in the conversation for the first time.

"Oh, I don't know if I should tell you that." Linda lowered her eyelashes.

"Maybe you shouldn't then," said Tommy quickly. He got up. "Come on, Linda, let's get going or we'll miss the start of the picture."

Linda uncrossed her legs reluctantly.

"Just a minute." Mrs. Jackson dried her hands.

"I think Linda knows something we ought to know," said Mr. Jackson.

"Dad, you'll be late for the start of your meeting," said Tommy. "Away you go to it and let Sadie alone."

"You're always covering up for that girl," said Mrs. Jackson, "but I'm her mother and I've a right to know what she's up to."

"Sadie's all right," said Tommy. "Let's go, Linda."

Linda got up and pushed back the chair. She looked round from one to the other. Her lower lip trembled slightly. "I don't want to cause any trouble."

"No, all right then, let's go." Tommy took hold of her arm.

Linda pulled it away and rubbed her elbow with her hand as if he had hurt her.

"Mind your manners, Tommy," said his father sharply.

Tommy's face closed tightly. He went to the window and stood looking into the small back yard. A patch of sunlight touched the dustbin but the rest was in shadow.

"Linda dear," said Mrs. Jackson, "now if there's anything you think we should know you must tell us."

Linda looked at Tommy's back. He did not move.

"That's right, Linda," said Mr. Jackson. "Your father wouldn't like it if you didn't."

"I suppose I'll have to, won't I?" Linda kept her eyes on Tommy. "I mean to say, what else can I do?" She paused. "She was with that Catholic boy Kevin McCoy."

Tommy wheeled round. "Kevin?"

"A Catholic boy?" said Mrs. Jackson in a stunned voice.

"Yes, the one Sadie and Tommy got mixed up with three summers ago, the one whose sister got hurt."

"Brede," said Tommy softly.

"That's the one," said Linda, not liking the look in Tommy's eye.

Mrs. Jackson eased herself into a seat by the table. She gripped the edge of the wood with her red, house-worn hands. "What's she doing with him?"

"How should I know? I just saw the two of them together waiting for a bus."

"Jim!" Mrs. Jackson appealed to her husband, who had been scratching his head and looking bewildered.

"What do you know about this, Tommy?" he demanded.

"Nothing." Tommy lifted his jacket. "I'm going to the pictures. You can come if you want to, Linda."

"Thanks very much!"

"This is a desperate shock, desperate." Mrs. Jackson rocked herself on the chair.

"For goodness sake, Ma, there's nothing in it," said Tommy. "Don't start going on about it as if she was about to marry him."

"Marry him?" His mother put her hand to her throat.

"She hasn't seen him for years."

"As far as you know."

"Tommy, go and get the brandy from the sitting room cabinet," said Mr. Jackson. "Your mother's just had a terrible shock."

Linda put her arm round Mrs. Jackson's neck. Tommy gritted his teeth and went through to the little sitting room at the front. It smelt musty as he opened the door. They seldom used it, only for Christmas and special company. The room was overstuffed with furniture and every ledge was covered with faded photographs and souvenirs brought from Portrush, Bangor and the Isle of Man. He opened the glass-fronted cabinet in which the best china was kept. He put his hand carefully round the back of a tea pot and brought out a half-bottle of brandy and a glass.

"You're a good girl, Linda," his mother was saying as he returned to the kitchen. "You've got your head screwed on."

Tommy splashed some brandy into a glass and gave it to his mother.

"You might have brought me one," said his father, "I've had a bit of a shock myself."

"I thought you were going to a Lodge meeting," said Tommy. "Is is not time you were away?"

"I've a brave excuse for being late the night. It's not every day you find your daughter's going out with a Taig."

"I'm sorry I let on," said Linda. "It just slipped out without me knowing it."

"Now don't worry, Linda," said Mrs. Jackson. "You did right to tell us."

"Come on, Linda, if you're coming." Tommy stood by the door.

Linda followed him. On the way out he heard his mother saying to his father, "I'm real glad Tommy's going out steady with such a nice girl as Linda." Linda heard it too though she did not bat an eyelash. Tommy shut the door behind them and they stood for a moment in the street, the small street of red brick terraced houses in which they had been born and brought up and played together.

Tommy began to walk; she caught up with him. She complained that he was walking too fast. He stopped when they were round the side of the house and looked at her.

"Why did you have to do that?"

"I didn't mean to." Her lower lip trembled.

"Oh, come off it, Linda, you knew you were going to tell them from the minute you walked in the door."

Linda's lip steadied. "Well," she said defiantly, "I think Sadie's a right eejit going with a Fenian."

"She's not going with him."

"How do you know?"

Tommy stood with his back to the wall with the mural of King Billy behind him, the mural that Kevin McCoy had once mutilated by writing DOWN WITH KING BILLY in white paint across it. It was the first time Linda had ever seen him angry and it made her feel a little afraid. He was usually very peaceable, much more so than Sadie.

"You don't know, do you?" said Linda. "I'm sure she doesn't tell you everything."

"She would have told me if she'd met Kevin again, I'm sure of that."

"You had a bit of a notion of his sister, hadn't you?"

"I did not. I just thought she was a nice girl."

"She's a Mick and she'll probably have twelve kids."

"What's that to do with it? I wasn't going to marry her. I was only fourteen at the time."

He began to walk again. Linda tagged along beside him but he was hardly aware of her. He was thinking about Brede's soft brown eyes and quiet smile. He had not thought of her for years. There was no point in thinking of her.

"Don't be angry with me." Linda's small warm hand crept into his. "I didn't mean any harm, honest I didn't, Tommy."

He sighed. "O.K."

"Shall we get some chocolate in Mrs. McConkey's before we go to the pictures?"

Mrs. McConkey kept a small shop in the next street. It sold everything from sweets to sticking plaster. She was reading the evening newspaper with her bosom resting on the counter. Every year her bosom increased until, as Sadie predicted, she might have to take on a larger shop to accommodate it.

"God help us, what times we're living in," she said, looking up as they came in. "It's time they were doing something about them louts."

She slapped the paper with her hand. "Clodding stones at the Army! Even the women and children are at it."

"I don't think they like getting their houses searched," said Tommy.

Mrs. McConkey lifted up her bosom from the counter and stared at him. "What side are you on anyway?"

"I was just making a comment."

"I think we'll have a couple of bars of milk chocolate, Mrs. McConkey," said Linda, pointing at the shelf. The continual talk of the Troubles bored her. As far as possible she didn't think about it. She wanted to enjoy herself. She didn't want to throw stones or have them thrown at her. They had done a bit of that when they were younger, but as her mother said, it was not she who had ever wanted to get mixed up in trouble like that, it was Sadie Jackson that had led her into it.

Chapter Three

Mrs. McCoy lifted the last soapy dish from the sink and laid it on the draining board for Brede to dry. Mr. McCoy sat in the corner muttering over the evening paper.

"Let them come and search this house!" he said. Mrs. McCoy said nothing. She wiped her hands on the towel and began to put the dishes away. "Why is it always Catholic houses they pick on, tell me that?" He looked at Brede demandingly.

Brede sighed.

"The British army has got to be run out of this province," he declared.

"There might be more trouble if they were," said Brede.

"You know nothing about it. You women are all the same. Peace at any price!"

Mrs. McCoy and Brede stacked the last of the dishes. The pile of plates was high as there were eight children in the family and next month there would be a ninth.

"Why don't you go and lie down, Ma?" said Brede. "You're looking tired."

"I'm all right. I'm just wondering where Kevin is. His tea's drying up in the oven."

"He'll come back sometime, don't worry."

Mrs. McCoy worried when he came in late, fearing the worst.

She worried when the younger children came in late too, for they roamed the district late at night in company with others taunting the soldiers who patrolled the streets. She made efforts to control them but was often too tired to do very much, and although their father disapproved in principle he did little about it. "Kids will be kids," he said. "Sure they're all the same. I'd have done the same at their age."

A loud sound like a gunshot made them all leap towards the door.

"Holy Mother of God!" said Mrs. McCoy, as she followed her husband and Brede out into the street.

Mr. McCoy was shaking his head and laughing. "Boys, Albert, you gave a queer fright for a minute there," he said.

"It's only Uncle Albert's car," said Brede to her mother.

Uncle Albert's car was rusty and ancient and her mother often declared it was only a miracle that it kept going at all and that it was a mystery to her as to why Albert should deserve such a miracle. He had eleven children at the last count and never did a day's work if he could avoid it. He lived on Social Security and sponged off his numerous brothers and sisters whenever that money ran out.

"Now listen, Pete," said Mrs. McCoy to her husband, "don't you be giving him anything. He never gave you back the last pound he borrowed. We've hardly enough to feed ourselves."

Albert got out of the car and joined them on the pavement.

"My, you're growing into a bonny girl, Brede," he said. "You'll be going up to the altar before we know it."

Brede blushed.

"She's time enough," said her mother sharply. "She might as well enjoy herself while she can."

"Aye, you didn't get much chance, did you, Mary?" said Albert.

"I'm not complaining."

Round the corner, on the opposite side of the road came a band of children, walking in single file, each carrying a toy gun or home-made weapon.

18

"There's our Gerald," said Brede.

Gerald was leading the line; further back walked two of the younger McCoys.

"Gerald," called his mother. "Come on you in."

"Oh Ma, it's early yet." Gerald halted with the line behind him.

"Let the lad alone," said his father. "It's a fine summer night, he's better out playing than sitting in the house."

"I don't like the games he's playing."

"Ach, all lads play at cops and robbers."

"There's a bit more than playing to what they're doing."

"Can you blame them when they see tanks touring the streets and soldiers with guns?"

Mrs. McCoy sighed. It was beyond her. She had not much time for the Protestants but she would have preferred to live in peace in her street and let them live in theirs and she did not see why there was any need to meet in the middle to fight. She wished she were back in the green fields of County Tyrone where she had grown up as a child. When she was little older than Brede, Pete McCoy, dark and handsome and curly-haired, with a fine persuading tongue on him, had come along and wooed her and brought her to the city. He had told her she would like the town, its bustle and excitement, but all she ever saw of it was this street of brick terraced houses and the main road beyond where she did her shopping. And instead of fishing for tiddlers or climbing trees her children played at death.

"Up the rebels!" shouted Albert.

He and his brother laughed and the children cheered. Gerald urged them on and away they went down the street, walking stealthily on the balls of their feet as if they were stalking an enemy.

"You've no call to encourage them like that, Albert," said Mrs. McCoy quietly.

"Sure you take everything too seriously," said Mr. McCoy. "Come on Albert, I think you and I'll take a wee trip down to the pub and have ourselves a jar."

Mrs. McCoy turned and went back to the house. Brede stood by the door watching her father and uncle get into the car. It careered off down the street back-firing loudly. It could have been the sound of gunfire. The sound made Brede freeze inside.

She returned to the kitchen where her mother now sat with a basket of mending at her feet. Her face was composed again though her eyes looked sad.

"Are you all right, Ma?" asked Brede. Mrs. McCoy laughed. "I thought I'd take a walk down the street and see Kate for a wee while."

"On you go, love. Don't be late," Mrs. McCoy added automatically. "And if you see Kevin tell him his tea's getting ruined."

The street was quiet. Brede walked quickly. As she came to the corner Gerald leapt out on her shouting, "Stick 'em up!" and pushed a wooden gun into her stomach.

She turned the gun aside. "For goodness sake, Gerald, one of these days you'll do it to the wrong person."

Gerald swung the gun from side to side pretending it was a machine gun, making a noise to represent the sound of its fire. Several of the other children slumped back against the wall clutching their chests and stomachs and sliding to the ground. On the wall was written in large letters UP THE I.R.A. and REMEMBER 1916.

Brede picked her way over the collapsed bodies of the children and carried on towards Kate's father's scrapyard. Kate and her family lived in a house beside it.

Kate was at home, sitting in her bedroom reading a magazine and allowing the polish to dry on her nails. She spent a great deal of time painting and polishing herself. She was pleased to see Brede.

"I was dead bored," she said. "There's nothing doing round this place."

"There's plenty doing in some ways." Brede leaned out of the window and looked back up the street. "Those kids worry me."

"Kids!" Kate blew on her nails. "We were just the same at their age."

"Not quite. They're much worse."

"We got into a bad fight ourselves once, you'll hardly be forgetting that."

"Hardly."

They had fought against a gang of Protestants and Brede had been badly hurt. She had been taken to hospital in an ambulance and Kevin had travelled behind in a police car with Sadie and Tommy Jackson, two of the Protestants. She thought about them now as she looked down on to the street and wondered what they would be doing.

She put her back to the window and leaned against the ledge.

"Have you seen Kevin at all?" she asked.

"Not since he left the yard. Has he not been home?"

Brede shook her head and shrugged. She was not really worried about him. He liked to wander far afield, hated to be confined within a few streets.

"I thought he might have been round to see me the night." said Kate. "He's not got another girl, has he?"

"Not as far as I know."

Kate tried to cling on to Kevin but most of the time she irritated him, and this Brede knew.

The voices from the street grew louder. Brede turned to look out of the window again. The children were running about excitedly.

She leaned out further and saw that two soldiers were coming down the road. Then an arm was raised and a brick went through the air.

"Trouble," she cried quickly and ran from the room.

She ran out of the house followed by Kate. Kate's mother was calling after them shouting to them to come back but they paid no attention. The children were all throwing stones now and anything else they could lay hands on. One of the soldiers had a streak of blood on the side of his head. They had both stopped dead, confronted by the children, their guns powerless in their hands. The soldiers looked young, no more than twenty years old.

For one moment they stood still, then they turned and ran.

"Yeller," screamed a child. "Cowardy cowardy custards!"

A cheer went up. They danced round and round yelling, brandishing their weapons above their heads.

"Fool!" cried Brede, seizing Gerald by the arm.

Gerald shook himself free and danced out of her reach. "Traitor," he shouted back at her.

"You've no right to be calling him a fool," said a voice behind her.

She wheeled round to see Brian Rafferty, an old friend of Kevin's, standing there. He was well over six feet tall now and had shoulders almost as wide as his father's. His father, Pat Rafferty, was well known in the district for his capacity for fighting. He had fists like hams and he raised them at the slightest provocation. Brian was becoming more and more like him.

"He's no fool to be fighting for his country."

"Fighting for his country! Brian Rafferty, you make me sick!"

"Brede McCoy, I never knew you had such a temper in you." Brian laughed softly. "I always thought you were that meek and mild."

"I'm not meek and mild when I see my young brother throwing bricks at soldiers."

"The soldiers are asking for it. They're occupying our country."

"It's not their fault. They'd probably rather be at home."

"Ah, give over arguing you two," said Kate, who was lounging against the wall. "Why don't we all go to the chippy and have a Coke? Kevin might be down there."

Brede looked at Gerald and said, "Go home at once, Gerald, or I'll send your da after you."

"Aye, away home now, you lot," said Brian. "And I'll see you tomorrow."

"Right, Brian," said Gerald. He saluted smartly, clicking his heels.

The children went at once. Brede watched them go wonderingly. Brian was looking very well pleased with himself.

"You haven't been encouraging them have you, Brian?" she asked slowly.

He laughed. He put his hands into his pockets and sauntered off down the street.

"I used to like him," said Brede. "Now I'm not sure. He's changed."

Kate yawned. "I heard he's got himself mixed up with the Provos."

"Surely not!"

The Provisionals were a splinter group from the Irish Republican Army. They were dedicated to the unification of Ireland and believed that they could only achieve their end by violence.

"Let's go down to the chippy," said Kate.

Brede shivered. "I'm cold. I'm going home."

She said good-night to Kate and ran all the way to her house. Her mother was still sitting in the kitchen mending. She looked up with a sock in her hand as Brede came in.

"What's up? Anything happened, Brede?"

"Have the kids come in?"

Mrs. McCoy nodded. "I've sent them up to bed."

Brede hesitated a moment.

She looked at her mother's tired face and knew that she could not give her anything more to worry about. She would talk to Kevin.

"Kevin hasn't been back?"

"No. Not a sign of him. Well, he'll just have to starve for his meal's burnt to a cinder."

Brede went up to the room that she shared with her three

23

sisters. They were in bed; one was asleep, the other two were playing cards. Brede took a book and sat by the window but she did not read. Every time she heard a step in the street she looked down to see if it was Kevin.

Chapter Four

Sadie and Kevin sat on the top of Cave Hill with the city spread out below them. They looked down at the great sprawl of factories, offices and houses that were gradually eating further and further into the green countryside beyond. Into the midst of the town came Belfast Lough. It was blue this evening, under a blue, nearly cloudless sky, speckled with ships and spiked by the shipyard gantries.

"I like looking down on the town," said Kevin.

"Me too," said Sadie. "It looks so peaceful. I wish it were!"

It was peaceful up there on the hill with the wind playing round their faces and tousling their hair. Sadie sat with her knees up to her chin, hugging her legs. She felt at ease with Kevin, though of course it was seldom she felt ill-at-ease with anybody, but she also felt a sort of contentment that she was unused to.

"It's funny," she began.

"What?" He turned on one elbow to look at her.

"I was just thinking a place looks better if you've got somebody with you."

"Two pairs of eyeballs are better than one. As long as they're the right two pairs of course."

He has a sweet tongue on him, she thought. He was gazing

back down at the city again. She stole a look at him. His face was not very broad but it was firm and had a suggestion of strength about it; it was also deeply tanned with the look of one who was seldom indoors. He probably went home only to sleep. She understood the feeling of restlessness in him. She had it herself.

He pointed down at the ships.

"Have you ever been in a boat, Sadie? A proper one?"

"No. Only a row boat at Bangor."

They both laughed.

"We'll go to Bangor one day again, will we?" said Kevin. "And I'll take you out in a row boat. I'll row you across the sea to Scotland. How would you like that?"

"I'd like it fine."

"You've devil enough in you for it, haven't you?"

Her eyes glinted. "My mother says I go out of the way to avoid the easy way round."

"If our mothers were to get together they would probably be saying the same things."

The words silenced them for they realised the impossibility of their mothers ever getting together.

"Well," said Kevin lightly, jumping to his feet, "will we go?" He held out his hand to her.

They walked down the hill close together but not touching. Lights were springing up in the houses, the blue in the sky was deepening and changing. Every moment it looked different; new colours and shades merged and infiltrated the blue: pinks, yellows, turquoise, red.

"Look at the sky," said Sadie. She felt she had never seen a sky before.

They stopped to look at it and Kevin rested a hand on her shoulder. His hand was warm and she liked the feel of it.

"It's a fair sight," said Kevin. "You never see it properly from the street."

He held her hand as they descended the last part of the hill and kept hold of it once they had reached the bottom.

"Would you like some chips?" he asked. "My stomach feels in need of something tasty."

They walked along the main road towards the centre of the city. He told her of some of the funny things they turned up in the scrap business, and she recounted some amusing tales of the women who shopped in the hat department.

He put his hand to touch her silky fair hair briefly. "I can't imagine you with a hat on your head."

They saw a Coca-Cola sign shining ahead and smelt the chips before they reached the café. They went inside. It was warm and bright and a juke box was playing. She sat down at an empty table, he went to the counter to get their order.

She glanced around her. The customers were nearly all teenagers sitting over cups of coffee and Coca-Cola. At the other side of the room she saw two girls she recognised: they worked in the same store. At the moment she saw them, they saw her too.

They got up and came across to her.

"Hi ya, Sadie. What are you doing round here?"

"I've been up the Cave Hill."

"On your lone?"

"No." She nodded towards Kevin where he stood in the queue.

They looked him over carefully and rolled their eyes in approval.

"Handsome looking fella. Where did you pick him up?"

"I didn't pick him up. I've known him a long time."

They examined him again with curiosity. The girls in the shop liked to spend their breaks talking about their boyfriends. Sadie seldom joined in for the talk bored her. They all had one thought in their minds: to get married as soon as possible.

Kevin came back carrying two plates of fish and chips. He set them down on the table. Sadie introduced him reluctantly to the girls who flashed bright smiles at him, but as soon as she said his name she could see their thoughts ticking over. Kevin McCoy. A Catholic name, unmistakably Catholic. Sadie stared them hard in the eyes, daring them to show anything they were thinking.

"Well, we'd better be getting along. See you the morn, Sadie."

They took another look at Kevin before they went out. They would be waiting for her in the cloakroom in the morning bursting with questions that she would not answer. There was no one better than Sadie Jackson at telling people to mind their own business.

Sadie laughed.

"What is it?" asked Kevin.

"Them two. They've got something to talk about all the rest of the way home."

"People have little to talk about," he said with disgust. "Come on, eat your fish and chips before they get cold."

Sadie discovered she was hungry after the fresh air up on the hillside. They ate quickly and then relaxed to drink their coffee. She asked him about the rest of his family.

"How many brothers and sisters do you have now?" she said. "I don't remember."

"There's eight of us altogether. One more than when I last saw you and there'll be another next month."

"Nine!" she said in horror. "What a life for your mother!"

"She's happy enough," he said shortly.

"Oh Kevin, don't be daft, what woman wants to wear herself out bringing up a load of kids like that?"

His face closed. He shrugged. He did not want to pursue it further but she would not let it die. She knew she was bad that way: often when it would be better to let something slide she went on determinedly.

"How can you ever expect to have a decent life if you go on having all those numbers of kids? I don't know why the Pope has to make you do it."

"You're talking rot." He was angry now. "The Pope doesn't make us. You Prods are all the same, you haven't the faintest idea what you're talking about."

They glared at one another across the table, then let their eyes fall. They did not want to fight, as they once had. Sadie swallowed hard before she spoke. She always found it difficult to withdraw.

"I'm sorry," she said. "I didn't really mean it like that."

"That's all right."

It was the first time since their meeting that evening that there was any unease between them. Kevin's brow was creased and his eyes were dark. Sadie fiddled with the spoon in her saucer.

"I wouldn't have nine kids myself, mind you," he said.

"No?"

"No. I couldn't feed them." He stood up. "Come on, I'll leave you home."

"You don't have to."

"I don't have to do anything. I never do anything I don't want to do. You should know that about me, Sadie Jackson."

She laughed and jumped up. "I know that. But it might be asking for trouble coming into my street."

"I'll leave you at the head of it, I won't come to your door. I wouldn't want to give your ma a heart attack."

They were friends again. They walked, hand in hand, through the streets, skirting the areas that were strung with barbed-wire barricades or that they knew might be troublesome. Once they had to take shelter in a doorway to get out of the path of two men. The men were running, feet clattering on the pavement, their breath gushing out in loud rasps. As they passed, Sadie and Kevin saw the look of the hunted in their faces. Seconds later four soldiers thundered by. When the noise of their feet had faded Sadie and Kevin went on their way. They walked with a feeling of closeness for they knew that they were inviting trouble in walking together at all.

Chapter Five

Mrs. Jackson was watching a film on television so she did not hear Mrs. Mullet coming into the house until she opened the kitchen door.

"I called out," said Mrs. Mullet, "but you didn't hear me."

"I was watching the telly," said Mrs. Jackson unnecessarily, her eyes still on it. The film had reached an exciting point and she was unwilling to put it off for the sake of Mrs Mullet whom she saw every day of her life. There were times when she wished the woman lived on the far side of Belfast. She had the longest tongue in the street and seemed to have little else to do all day but lean against her door jamb and wait for passers-by with whom she could trade bits of news. The news nearly always tended to be rumours, and usually scandalous. Mrs. Mullet was frequently declaring herself horrified.

She stood by the kitchen door now, in her high spiky-heeled shoes, of the kind that had ceased to be fashionable years ago. It was not that Mrs. Jackson was fashionable herself, but Mrs. Mullet liked to pride herself on her clothes sense.

"I'll take the weight off me feet," she said. "Me legs are killing me the day. I've never been off the go."

"Sit down for a minute then." Mrs. Jackson got up and

turned down the sound of the television to a low murmur, but kept the picture as it was.

Mrs. Mullet collapsed into Mr. Jackson's armchair and kicked off her shoes. "That's better."

Mrs. Jackson eyed her suspiciously. She had either come to gossip, or to borrow. A quarter pound of tea here and a couple of eggs there. She lived off the street, Mrs. Jackson had often remarked to her husband; it was no wonder she could forever be affording to buy new clothes for herself and Linda. She came often these days to talk about Tommy and Linda. She liked Tommy, thought he was a nice steady lad, and was hoping for a match. Mrs. Jackson was hoping that Tommy would have more sense.

"Tommy's out with Linda tonight then," said Mrs. Mullet. Mrs. Jackson was not looking at her; she was watching the moving figures on the screen. "They seem right fond of each other."

"They're very young."

"Kids are getting married younger all the time."

Mrs. Jackson looked at her now. "More fool them!"

"Oh, come now, Mrs. Jackson, what a thing to say! Why shouldn't they if that's what they want."

"They want to see a bit of life first instead of getting tied down to a wife and a couple of kids."

Mrs. Mullet pursed her lips. "I married at seventeen and I can't say I've ever regretted it."

"Are you wanting a cup of tea?" asked Mrs. Jackson, determined to have no more of the subject.

"Wouldn't say no."

Mrs. Jackson put on the kettle and laid out a few biscuits on a plate.

"Sadie out too the night?"

Mrs. Jackson's back stiffened. "Well, she's not in."

"Linda saw her on the way home."

Mrs. Jackson infused the tea and set it on a low gas. She

placed two cups on the draining board. "You take milk and sugar, don't you, Mrs Mullet?"

"Two sugars please. Yes, Linda was saying she saw Sadie waiting on a bus."

Mrs. Jackson poured the tea and gave a cup to Mrs. Mullet. Then she sat herself down and faced the television squarely. "Would you like to see the film?"

"Not particularly. I've seen it before anyway."

They drank their tea and ate biscuits to the low accompanying hum of the television set. Mrs. Jackson was bracing herself for the next remark.

"I know it's none of my business, Mrs. Jackson, but I wouldn't like Sadie to get into any harm—"

Mrs. Jackson cut her off. "That's all right, Mrs. Mullet. You don't need to worry about Sadie for me. She's got her head screwed on."

"There's been times when it seems to come a bit loose. Oh, I'm not criticising her, don't think that for a minute. You know I'm right fond of her and she and Linda have been as thick as thieves since they were in the cradle."

Mrs. Jackson rose and turned up the volume of the television. The film was a Western and the sound of gunshots and galloping hooves drowned out the voice of Mrs. Mullet.

The door scraped open and Mr. Jackson put his head round it. "I'm back, Aggie. Oh hello there, Mrs. Mullet, how are you?"

"Not so bad."

"You'll be wanting your supper?" Mrs. Jackson said to her husband.

"Could do with a cup of tea at any rate. Your husband's home from the meeting now, Mrs. Mullet. Looking for his supper too, I bet."

"You men never think of anything but your stomachs!" Mrs. Mullet got up. "I'll be seeing you."

She went out.

Mrs. Jackson turned the television sound right down. "That

woman gives me the dry bokes!"

Mr. Jackson laughed and rubbed his hands together. He had had a pint of Guinness on the way back from the meeting and was in good form.

"Aggie, what a thing to say! I heard you telling Sadie off the other day for using the word."

"I'd tell her off if she was here right now. The trouble she gets us in to! She's always causing talk in this street, Jim, and it's time she was stopping it. I'm sick of that Mullet woman coming over here to tell me the latest gossip about Sadie."

"Ah, Sadie's all right."

"Hanging about with a Mick? Do you not mind that?"

Mr. Jackson's face sobered. "I mind that all right. But there may be nothing to it. We've only got Linda's word for it and I wouldn't take her word for gospel."

Linda's mother closed the front door behind her after hearing the first part of the Jacksons' conversation. So old woman Jackson was sick of her coming over, was she? Mrs. Mullet tossed her head. She'd not let that pass. She would see to it that the street knew what was going on and would have no qualms about it. There was nothing wrong in telling the truth, and they had to protect themselves from Catholic infiltrators. That's why their men went to their Lodges and walked in parades: they were defending their faith. She crossed the street. There was no one in sight except for four small boys playing at soldiers. They were wearing khaki anoraks and soldiers' berets that they had filched somewhere. She went into her own house to tell the story to Mr. Mullet. He was reading the greyhound racing results in the evening paper and seemed more interested in them than the treachery of Mrs. Jackson.

"She's a decent enough woman," was all he said.

"My Gawd, you men! What would you say if our Linda was walking out with a Mick?"

"But she's not, is she?" he said mildly, not even lifting his head. "Tommy's a good Protestant even if he doesn't belong to the Lodge."

Mrs. Mullet returned to the doorway where she stood watching the light failing over the street. The only person she saw was old Granny McEvoy, wrapped in her grey shawl, out looking for her cat. But Granny McEvoy was almost stone deaf and got the whole story wrong so Mrs. Mullet gave up in despair. She had to put up with ten minutes of the old woman telling her how her man had fought with the Specials at the time of the partition of Ireland, and escaped death by inches. Mrs. Mullet had heard the story so often that she could have retold it backwards.

"He was a real patriot," said Granny, gathering her shawl around her. "And now you're telling me we've got Micks living in this street?"

"No, no, Granny, away ye go and get your cat. That wasn't what I was saying at all."

Granny shuffled off calling for the cat. Mrs. Mullet looked up the street thinking it was time that Tommy and Linda were coming home. The pictures would have finished half an hour ago at least.

Tommy and Linda were sitting in a café drinking coffee. Linda had enjoyed the film, she had had a good cry at one point, but Tommy had been bored. He supposed that was part of the price you had to pay when you took a girl out. He quite liked taking Linda out. She could be very soft and sweet, and it was nice to sit in the cinema holding her hand.

"Here's Steve," said Linda.

Steve was Tommy's friend from schooldays. He was rather keen on Sadie but she said he bored her, he had no imagination. It was seldom that she went out more than twice with any boy.

"Can I join you?" said Steve.

"Sure." Tommy pulled up a chair.

Steve sat down.

"We've been to the pictures," said Linda.

"Guess where I've been?" said Steve to Tommy. "I've joined the Lodge."

Tommy said nothing.

"I keep telling Tommy he ought to join," said Linda. "After all most of the men round here belong. I'd like to see him walking on the 'Twelfth'."

Tommy shrugged.

"Why don't you, Tommy?" said Steve. "You could still play in the band."

Tommy had once wanted to play the flute in the Junior Pipe Band, but that was before the fight in which Brede had almost been killed. That night when they thought she might die he had decided not to walk in the Orange parade. Both Linda and Steve knew that, though neither could understand it, and he could not quite explain it. It was not as if he had changed his allegiance: he would never do that. As far as he was concerned, Ulster must stay British and Protestant.

"Sure it's good crack apart from anything else," said Steve.

"I like the 'Twelfth'," said Linda. "The bands playing and all that."

"I think we should be getting home, Linda," said Tommy.

"You're a stubborn one, aren't you?" said Linda.

"I think perhaps he isn't much of a Loyalist when it comes to the bit," said Steve. "There's times when you have to stand up and be counted."

Tommy stood up. "Are you coming, Linda?"

She followed him out. "You don't even speak up for yourself," she said with annoyance.

"I don't see why I should, Steve doesn't have to tell me what to do."

"But the other men won't like it, Tommy, if you don't join in with them."

"Why should I care about that? Anyway, not everybody belongs to the Orange Order just because they're Protestants. Lots of lads in the yard don't."

"But most of the men in the street do."

"Forget it, Linda," he said quietly.

"All right," she sighed.

He saw Sadie and Kevin ahead before Linda did. For a minute he thought of wheeling Linda about and taking her back along the road but it was too late. She had seen them too.

"Isn't that Sadie?" she said excitedly.

Sadie and Kevin were standing at the end of the street. They turned as Tommy and Linda approached.

"Hello, you two." Sadie's voice was loud and defiant.

"Hello, Tommy," Kevin spoke more quietly.

"Hello, Kevin."

For a moment there was silence. Tommy and Kevin looked at one another, each wishing to speak, not knowing what to say.

"How've you been?" asked Kevin at last.

"Fine."

There was a further silence and then Tommy said, "How's Brede?"

"O.K."

"Tell her I was asking for her."

"I will." Kevin scuffed his foot against the edge of the kerb. "Well, I suppose I'd better be going. Nice to see you again, Tommy." He nodded at Linda. "Good-night, Sadie."

"Good-night, Kevin," said Sadie.

He walked quickly away.

"He'd need to walk fast in case any of our boys get the hold of him," said Linda.

"You shut up, Linda Mullet," said Sadie.

"Why should I shut up?" demanded Linda.

"Pack it in, both of you," said Tommy.

"You don't seem to care that your sister's been going with a Mick." Linda tossed her head. Tommy knew he had nettled her by sending his regards to Brede.

"Let's go," he said. As they came down the street they saw the shape of Mrs. Mullet outlined in her lit doorway. "And don't you say anything to your ma, Linda."

"I'll say what I like."

"If you do you won't see me again."

"That'll make her stop to think," said Sadie. "She doesn't want to lose you now she's got her claws in you."

Linda flew at Sadie. Tommy separated them. "For heaven's sake, cut it out!" He cursed Sadie under his breath. She had the devil in her at times.

Mrs. Mullet crossed the street. "What's going on here?"

"Nothing, Mrs. Mullet," said Tommy.

"We were just coddin', Mrs. Mullet," said Sadie with false sweetness in her voice.

Linda was quiet.

"Would you like a cup of tea?" asked Mrs. Mullet. "I've got one on the gas now."

"No thanks," said Tommy. "I've to be up for my work in the morning."

"See you tomorrow, Tommy?" said Linda.

"Aye, good-night."

He and Sadie left Linda and her mother. When they heard the Mullets' door shut, Sadie said, "There's times when I could spit in that woman's eye. And what you see in Linda I'll never know!"

"Oh give over, Sadie," said Tommy wearily, feeling he had had enough of women for one day. "You'd think you might have learned to keep your mouth shut."

"You're all for a quiet life."

"You're in a real aggressive mood."

She shrugged and then said, "I'm getting ready for the storm. I've no doubt that Linda has brought the news home about Kevin and me."

The storm broke as soon as they came into the kitchen. Sadie stood with her head up listening to her mother's tirade. At the end of it she said, "All I've done is go for a walk with a boy."

"*All?*" said her mother.

"You're not seeing him again, do you hear?" said her father.

"I'll see him if I want to." Sadie opened the kitchen door.

"Come you back here," roared her father.

She hesitated. Mr. Jackson walked across to her. He put his hands on her shoulders.

"You'll do what I tell you as long as you're living under my roof."

"I don't have to stay under your roof. I'm sixteen, going on seventeen. I can go if I want to. You can't get the police to bring me back."

Mrs. Jackson caught her breath. Sadie eased herself out of her father's grasp and walked up the stairs. He made to follow her but his wife said quietly, "Let her be, Jim. She's headstrong, you'll only turn her against you."

Tommy shut the door. His mother sniffed and wiped her eyes with the back of her hand.

"That girl needs taught a lesson," said Mr. Jackson.

"I don't think there's anything to it, Da," Tommy said. "She just met Kevin by chance."

"But what's she going to do now, that's what I'd like to know?" said his mother. "I hope she won't see him again. You go on up and talk to her, Tommy. Maybe she'll listen to you."

Tommy found Sadie sitting on her bed. He closed the door and sat down beside her.

"Don't do anything stupid, Sadie."

"What are you trying to say?"

"I don't think you should see Kevin again."

"That's up to me, isn't it?"

"Look, you know that I like Kevin. He's a nice fellow but if you start to go out with him it'll just lead to trouble. Look how much there's been already."

Sadie got up and walked to the window. She opened it and leaned out. "I'm sick of this street and all the people in it. I'm going to make up my own mind. There was a time when you agreed, Tommy. We spent some good days together, the four of us, didn't we?"

He stirred uneasily. "But it became difficult, didn't it? We always had to slip away, pretend we were going somewhere else. We had to give it up."

"Perhaps we gave up too easily." Her voice was quiet now, all aggression gone from it. "Perhaps that's why things are in such a bad way."

"You're not going to change anything by going out with Kevin McCoy."

He left her still leaning out of the window looking down on the street. She stayed there for a long time, with her elbows on the sill, thinking of Kevin's dark eyes and infectious laugh. The thought of him stayed with her whilst she got ready for bed and eventually fell asleep.

Chapter Six

Kevin opened the kitchen door briefly, announced that he was back, and closed it before his mother and father could ask him where he had been. He went upstairs quietly for all the children would be in bed, most of them fast asleep. He heard one or two grunts and heavy breathing as he reached the top step.

"You're late."

Brede was standing on the landing in her pyjamas.

"Not that late," Kevin whispered back. "I've been later."

"You didn't come in for your tea. Ma was worried."

He sighed, wishing that his mother could stop worrying about him. He was nearly eighteen after all and she had seven younger than him to concern herself with. But then he knew that all mothers in this part of Belfast worried about their sons when they came home late. They often had cause to.

"Want to know where I've been?"

"Where, Kevin?" asked Brede swiftly.

"Oh, nowhere dangerous. Do you think I've been holed up in a Provo hide-out or something?"

"Of course not," she said, but there was a slight trace of doubt in her voice. It was always a possibility that a boy of his age would get involved either by desire or accident with the

Irish Republican Army or the Provisionals. "Is it a secret?"

"Yes."

She came closer to him. "You can trust me."

"I know that or I wouldn't tell you."

"Let me guess. You were out with a girl?"

"That's right."

"I shan't tell Kate."

"Kate! I'm not bespoke to her."

Brede laughed softly. "Go on then, tell me. Do I know her?"

"You did once. Three years ago."

"Not Sadie!"

He chuckled. "How did you guess?"

"She came into my mind earlier for some reason or other."

They were quiet as they heard the kitchen door open and Mr. McCoy go to the front door to lock it for the night. Their parents went in to the front room and prepared for bed. The low sound of their voices floated up to them. After a few minutes there was a creaking of bed springs, and then silence.

They spoke more quietly now. Kevin told Brede of his meeting with Sadie and how they had gone up on Cave Hill.

"Are you seeing her again?" she asked.

"I'm taking her to Bangor on Saturday."

She sighed. "Should you, do you think?"

"Ah, Brede! There's an awful lot of things nobody should do these days." He yawned. "I'm goin' to bed."

He fell asleep at once. He could sleep standing up, as Brede often said, but she did not sleep so easily. She lay awake for a while watching the reflection of the street light through the thin curtains. She lay thinking of Sadie and Tommy. She wouldn't mind seeing Tommy again but knew she would not. She saw too much trouble all around her to want to cause any more.

The McCoy household stirred early in the morning. Mrs. McCoy was up first, feeding the baby, and then her husband who was working at present on a building site, and Kevin who started early in the scrapyard. Brede usually rose early, too, to help. Her mother often said that she did not know what she would do without her and that when she married it would be like losing her right hand.

"There's your pieces," said Mrs. McCoy to her husband and Kevin, setting two plastic boxes of sandwiches on the kitchen table.

Kevin took his box and went off down the street whistling. It was a fine morning and the birds were chirping from the roof-tops. He liked being out before too many people were astir.

As he came abreast of the Raffertys' doorway Brian came out pulling on his jacket.

"Take your time, Kevin. I'll walk down with you."

"Brian," screeched Mrs. Rafferty from inside the house, "if you see that father of yours you can tell him he needn't bother coming home again."

She appeared in the doorway in curlers and dressing gown. She had the shrillest voice in the street, and that was quite a claim.

Kevin took a few steps away.

"Good morning, Kevin," she said, noticing him. "Honest, that man of mine is a cross no woman should have to bear! He'll never put foot over this doorstep again if I have anything to do with it."

"For goodness sake, Ma!" Brian said "You know fine enough you'll have him in." He fell into step beside Kevin and they left her raving to herself. "He'll be back as soon as he plucks up enough courage to face her." He chuckled. "She's the only one he's afeard of."

There was a time when Kevin had stood in awe of Pat Rafferty, six foot four and as broad as an ox, a man who was ready to fight and afraid of nobody. Except his wife. Kevin had always overlooked that. Now Pat Rafferty bored him, and when the man was drunk he thought he was just stupid. There were times too now that Brian bored him, and this bothered

42

him a bit for they had been friends all their lives.

They turned along the road that led to the scrapyard.

"I'll come along with you," said Brian. "I've plenty of time."

Kevin glanced at him sideways. "What's on your mind?"

"You're a good patriot, aren't you, Kevin? You always have been."

"That's right enough."

"You believe in the cause?"

"Well, of course I do, you know that. I'm a republican."

They had reached the gate of the yard. Kate's father was already moving around inside it sorting out bits of junk. Kevin raised his hand in greeting.

Brian put his hand on Kevin's arm and said in a low voice, "We have to be prepared to fight for what we believe in, Kevin." No response came from Kevin so Brian added, "Are you ready to fight?"

"I don't see what good it would do."

"You can't mean that."

Kevin shrugged.

"Kevin," Kate's father called, "come and give us a hand. I can't get this thing moved."

"Just coming, Mr. Kelly."

"Meet me later, Kevin," said Brian urgently. "It's important."

"Kevin," called Mr. Kelly again. "I'm going to drop this blasted thing on me foot if you don't come soon."

"Must go." Kevin dashed off.

"See you later," Brian shouted after him.

Kevin helped release Mr. Kelly who was half-pinned under the twisted chassis of a car.

Mr. Kelly wiped the sweat from his brow. He was a small stocky man with amazing strength in his arms. Years of lifting junk had developed his muscles. Carry on in this business, Kevin, he was always saying, and you'll end up as strong as an ox, and there's nothing a girl likes better than a man with big muscles. Then he would wink knowingly, and in front of

Kevin's eyes would float a vision of Kate. There were times when he was tempted to give in his notice but work was not all that easy to come by, unemployment was high, and they needed the money at home.

"I thought you were going to stand there all day bletherin' to Brian Rafferty. He's turning into a right hallion. I would watch yourself there if I were you, Kevin boy."

"Ach, Brian's all right. Full of hot air at times, that's all."

"Just like his da, eh?"

They laughed.

They set off in the old truck in which they collected the scrap. They drove out into one of the suburbs. Trees and flowers bloomed in the well-kept gardens. There were no barbed-wire barricades here or burnt-out cars or words scrawled on gable-ends of houses. All was peaceful. Not even a soldier about, and only an occasional policeman walked, quite relaxed compared with the ones that trod the beat in their streets.

"Sure it's peaceful here, Kevin," sighed Mr. Kelly.

Kevin agreed, though he was not sure he could have lived in one of those neat villas screened by a hedge with a tidy lawn in front. He could not actually see himself inside it. The trouble at the moment was that he could not see himself anywhere. His own house did not hold him either.

They covered the area, going from house to house, taking their time. Mr. Kelly was not one for rushing about, and at lunchtime he disappeared for an hour into a pub and left Kevin to guard the truck. Kevin sat on the back in the sun leaning against the tail-board enjoying the warmth on his face. He thought of Sadie and that made him smile, but when he thought of Brian he was uneasy. He was not at all sure that Brian was all right.

They stayed out till fairly late that evening. Neither of them was in a mood for going home. "The women are never done fussing," said Mr. Kelly. "You and I might as well enjoy our bit of peace while we have it, Kevin."

He dropped Kevin off at the end of his street. They would

unload in the morning. "As well then as tonight," said Mr. Kelly, and Kevin agreed.

When he came into the kitchen he saw Brian sitting in the corner waiting for him.

"You're late the night," said his mother.

"Sure is he ever early?" said his father.

"I've been waiting on you this half hour," said Brian.

"Lay off, the lot of you," said Kevin, sitting down at the place set for him at the table. "I've been working."

"Idling round the streets, if I know Dan Kelly," said Mr. McCoy. "And that reminds me, it's time you were asking him for a rise."

"How can he give me a rise?"

"He was supposed to be making a fortune when you went to work for him," said Mrs. McCoy.

"Well, business is slacker now."

Kevin began to eat. He was wishing he hadn't bothered coming home at all but had taken a turn round by the City Hall at the same time as last night. Brian was fidgeting with a box of matches, turning them over and over in his hand. As soon as Kevin had finished his meal, Brian said, "Are you right then, Kevin?" He made for the door.

"Where are you two off to?" asked Mrs. McCoy.

"Nowhere in particular," said Brian.

Kevin followed Brian out. "Where *are* we going?" he asked, when they were in the street.

"To my house. I've something to show you."

Brian's mother was out at the Bingo and his father sat in front of the television set looking very subdued. He was nursing a sore head. Brian said he had had too much drink in him the night before and ended up in a fight.

"Come on," said Brian. "Up the stairs."

They went up to Brian's room and he closed the door. He was grinning as he looked at Kevin. "You'll never guess what I've got under the bed?"

"A stick of dynamite," said Kevin sarcastically.

"You're getting near."

"*What*?" Kevin frowned. "Brian, what have you got?"

Brian knelt down and pulled a box from under the bed. Kevin crouched beside him. He watched as Brian lifted the lid and removed old newspapers that were lying on top. Underneath was a rifle and several rounds of ammunition.

"Whew!" said Kevin softly.

"Well, what do you say to that then?" Brian sat back on his heels with pride. "Surprised you, didn't I?"

"You're a nit, Brian."

"Very funny."

Brian, in a sudden blaze of temper very like his father's, seized Kevin by the shirt. Kevin pushed him backwards and he went reeling against a chest of drawers. Brian was heavier but Kevin's arms were stronger. Brian got to his feet ready to lunge again at Kevin.

"Quit it, Brian," said Kevin. "It'll do no good the two of us fighting."

Brian's shoulders slumped. The fire was gone out of him. He sat down on the bed.

"How the hell do you think you can hide a rifle when the army could be round here any time searching?" demanded Kevin.

"I'll have to find a better place. I'm not going to keep it here."

"And where do you think you'll find it?"

"I had ould Kelly's yard in mind."

"Not on your life! Kelly'd have a fit."

"There must be dozens of places in that ould yard that even he wouldn't think of looking in. There's rubbish there that he hasn't turned over for years. You'd know a good place, Kevin."

"No," said Kevin abruptly.

"So you're not going to help?"

"I don't want anything to do with guns. It's madness."

"That's not the way you once talked. There was a time when you were full of strong talk about fighting to get the six coun-

46

ties back from England. Up the Rebels! What's happened to all that now?"

"I was younger then."

"Some excuse that!"

"You've no call to speak to me like that, Brian Rafferty." Kevin's temper was rising now. "There's enough people getting killed. I want nothing to do with it."

"Coward!"

"Take that back!" Kevin seized Brian by the shirt.

"Why the hell should I?"

"Brede almost died. Remember!"

"But she's all right now, isn't she?"

Kevin shoved Brian away from him. They had fought often as boys but if they were to fight now it would be much more serious.

"Where did you get that lot, Brian?"

"Do you think I'd tell you that?" Brian stood up beside him. "Look, Kevin, why don't you join us? You want one Ireland, you do, don't you. There's no other way but this. There's not, you know it yourself."

"I'm not afraid of fighting if I see a need for it, but I'm not for people dying."

"But it's the enemy that'll die," cried Brian.

"You're not such an eejit as to believe that." Kevin shook his head. "If there's bullets flying your mother could be standing in the road, or mine."

He walked over to the door.

"So you won't be one of us?" said Brian slowly. "Traitor!"

"Call me what you like. There's dozens of Catholics who aren't one of you either, and don't you forget that!"

Brian caught him by the arm. "If you let on, you know what'll happen to you."

"I won't let on, I'm no stool pigeon." Kevin shook himself free. "But be careful what you do with that damned thing. You might blow your own head off with it. You're thick enough."

47

He opened the door and went quickly down the stairs. At the foot he looked back up at Brian, who was standing on the top step. Brian held the rifle in his hands pointed down at him.

Brian laughed softly. "Scared?"

Kevin turned his back on him and walked out through the front door into the street.

Chapter Seven

Sadie and Kevin rode to Bangor on the top deck of the bus, in the front seat. The countryside looked lush and pretty; the trees were in leaf and sprays of pink and yellow blossom lingered here and there.

The resort was not busy: it was too soon in the year for holiday-makers. The local inhabitants moved in and out of the shops getting in their stores for the weekend.

Sadie and Kevin walked along by the sea wall enjoying the smell of the sea. The breeze whipped back their hair and tinged their cheeks with pink.

"It's good to be out of the town," said Sadie with a little skip.

They walked round the bay as far as Pickie Pool, the outdoor swimming pond. They had brought their bathing costumes.

"It looks icy cold to me," said Kevin, staring down at the green water. "I'm not sure I fancy it much."

"Oh come on, Kevin. Once we're wet it'll be O.K."

Kevin looked doubtful. "It's all right for you. Women have an extra layer of fat on them. They don't feel the cold so much." But he went off to change and reappeared to join her a few minutes later.

"The first bathe of the year," said Sadie, as they stood at the side of the pool.

"We must be mad going swimming in May. This isn't the Riviera."

"We're mad anyway," laughed Sadie, and in a flash she was up on her toes and diving in neatly. She surfaced gasping.

"You look like you've dived into the Arctic Ocean," said Kevin, still hovering on the edge.

"Coward!" Her teeth chattered.

That brought him in. She swam away from him with strong even strokes; he pursued her in a fast sprawling crawl. He caught her by the shoulders.

"What was that you said?"

"You're the bravest man this side of the Boyne."

"The Boyne? I'm not fond of the Boyne." The Boyne was where King William had fought and defeated the Catholics under James II. "Let's say the Shannon."

Sadie could say nothing more. Her lips were blue. They swam a length and then clambered up out of the water.

"God, let's get out," said Kevin.

They dressed and went into the restaurant to drink hot chocolate. As they drank, heat gradually returned to their bodies.

"Boys, I thought the shock would kill me," said Kevin. "Who's idea was that anyway?"

"I thought you were one for a challenge?"

He grinned back at her. "I'd hardly be here if I weren't, would I? There's a few in my street would be having a heart attack if they could see us now."

"Let's forget about your street," said Sadie, "and mine."

"A good idea that."

They walked round the path beside the sea. They met no one. It was as if they had the whole world to themselves. "Wouldn't it be nice if we did?" said Sadie. They sat on the rocks and spun stones through the waves vying with one another to see who could throw furthest.

"You've got a good throw for a girl," said Kevin. "They're usually hopeless." Sadie threw another stone skimming it closely through the waves. "You must have known the wrong girls," she said.

At midday she unpacked her bag. She had made up a picnic after her mother had gone to bed the night before. Ham and cheese sandwiches, cold sausages, crisps, little sponge cakes and a bottle of Coca-Cola.

"Fancy you being domesticated," said Kevin, watching with admiration.

"I'm not. But I like my grub."

They were ravenously hungry after their bathe. They ate everything. "There was supposed to be enough there for our tea as well," said Sadie.

"Who cares? I'll buy you a meal in a café. I'm loaded."

"So you're rich, eh?"

"Yesterday was pay day. By Monday most of it'll be spent. That's the way it goes."

That was the way it went for her too. They kept finding things on which they agreed, attitudes they shared.

They returned to the town and their mood changed again. They sampled the amusement arcades playing the pin ball and fruit machines and even trying their luck at the shooting gallery. Kevin proved to be a good shot. Sadie watched his concentration as he lined up his target, his dark eyes intense, his hand steady. He won first prize.

"You're a dab hand with a gun," she said.

And then he thought of Brian with a gun hidden under his bed and of him standing with it in his hands at the top of the stairs, and he frowned.

"What's wrong?" asked Sadie.

"Nothing. Let's go."

He led the way out of the arcade and she followed, puzzled. But outside he smiled again and she forgot the look of blackness on his face. She lived in the present too much to worry about even the moment before.

51

"Candy floss, madam?" He presented her with a large mound of pink froth.

They visited the harbour to look at the boats, hesitating for a long time over the one they would choose in which to sail round the world.

He took her hand and led her on again. The day was endless, full of delight and variation. A day of bright sky and white-tipped green water and seagulls wheeling overhead.

After they had eaten at tea-time they wandered round the bay to Ballyholme and went down on to the sands. They found a sheltered place in which they could sit shielded from the wind. Sadie took off her sandals and rubbed her feet in the sand.

"I feel happy," she said.

"Me too." Kevin lay back with his hands clasped behind his head. She rolled on to her stomach and looked down at his face. "Funny we should get on so well together."

"Funny?"

"Well, you know what I mean. With so many things against it."

"Only one. And that doesn't seem to matter."

"No. Not when we're together."

"Does it bother you when we're not?"

"I don't know. In a way. I find it odd when I think about you going to things like—" she paused "—confession."

"It's part of my religion."

"It's a part I don't like, Kevin. Would you confess to the priest that you were going with a Protestant girl?"

He sat up. "There's no law against it. It's not a mortal sin."

"I hate that word sin."

He shrugged.

She sat up too and looked him in the face. "Don't you resent the power the priests have over you?"

"They don't have that much power," he muttered.

"Of course they do," she insisted.

"You know nothing about it." His voice had a hard edge.

Give over, a voice inside her was saying, but the stubbornness in her would not let it lie.

"And those statues and things. I don't know how you can bring yourself to pray to them."

"Aye, and what about your lot?" His temper was surging. "Worshipping a silly old Dutchman dead these three hundred years."

"We don't worship him."

"Ah, for God's sake!" He stood up. "King Billy on his white horse. Long Live King Billy! Keep the Micks down!"

"If there were more of you than there were of us you'd soon keep us down." Sadie's eyes blazed. Her father's words, cut into her mind.

"So you're afraid, that's what it is!" He laughed contemptuously, and at that moment she hated him.

He turned on his heel and walked away. She let him go. She watched until he was out of sight. Now she was alone on the sands. The sky was covered with grey cloud, the sun gone for the day. A spot of rain touched her cheek. She sat with her chin on her knees glowering at the grey water. Their beautiful day was spoiled.

Another spot of rain. Let it pour. She did not care if she was soaked and caught pneumonia and died. Maybe then he would be sorry. He was no better than the rest of them.

The rain began to come down, first in a fine drizzle and then in a solid sheet. She felt hands on her shoulder pulling her up.

"Stupid twit!" he shouted at her and hauled her across the darkening sand. They ran to a shelter and once inside, stood there panting, looking at one another. Sadie's hair hung in long wet strands to her waist.

"Get your towel out and dry yourself," he said, and she did so.

She took off her anorak and he shook it vigorously. He looked angry yet, his eyes were black and there was no hint of a smile. He must hate her, she thought.

53

"Did you want to catch your death out there?" he demanded.

She shook her head. She swallowed deeply and then she said, "I'm sorry."

His mouth softened. "That's all right. I'm sorry too."

"No, no, it was my fault. I have a terrible tongue on me at times, my mother's always telling me."

He laughed, put out his hand and smoothed her hair. "It was all silly anyway."

She nodded. "I'm glad you came back for me."

There was a time when he would have been too proud to go back but when he had returned and seen her crouching on the wet beach he knew he could not walk away.

"Did you think I'd leave you sitting there all alone on the sands?"

He helped her put her anorak on and laid his hands on her shoulders. "You look like a drowned rat," he said and then he kissed her.

She moved nearer to him. She linked her hands round the back of his neck and rested her cheek against his sweater. Outside the rain beat down, hissing on the pavement, drumming on the roof of their shelter. They stayed there until it ceased, holding one another close. It was time then to go for the last bus home. They walked through the wet streets, arms around one another's waists, feeling dazed and damp, but not caring about the dampness.

As they came into the bus station they saw the rear end of the Belfast bus sliding away. Kevin broke free from her and ran after it shouting, but the bus gathered speed and was soon heading for the open road leaving them behind.

"Last bus, son," said a conductor, who was on his way homewards.

"Sadie," said Kevin with mock solemnity, "that was the last bus."

"I don't care," she said dreamily. "We could go back and sit on the sand."

"And get washed away with the tide! We'll have to try and hitch a lift."

They set out on the road. Kevin thumbed several cars but they swept past with their lights blazing. It was not easy to get a lift at night. Drivers were wary of picking up strangers these days. They walked fairly briskly to keep themselves warm and as they walked they sang. He sang 'The Wearing of the Green' and she sang 'The Sash My Father Wore' and then they laughed together.

"Our parents would have a fit if they could hear us," said Kevin.

"Hey, just a minute, here's another car coming and it's not travelling as fast."

It chugged towards them. What it lacked in speed it made up for in noise. Kevin held up his thumb. It stopped.

"Hurrah!" shouted Sadie.

Kevin led her to the car and opened the passenger door. He peered inside to have a word with the driver.

"Glory be!" he said. "It's Uncle Albert."

Chapter Eight

Uncle Albert peered back. "Is that you, Kevin boy?"

"It is."

"What are you doing out here at this time of the night?"

"Looking for a lift."

The engine shuddered and died. "Blast it," said Uncle Albert. "This is a pig to start once it stops."

"I know that!" said Kevin. "Uncle Albert, I've a friend here with me. This is Sadie. Sadie, this is my father's brother."

Uncle Albert leaned over to take Sadie's hand. "Pleased to meet you, Sadie."

"How do you do, Mr. McCoy."

"Are you getting in then, the two of you?"

"We'll get in the back," said Kevin.

"And then you can have a wee cuddle, eh?" Uncle Albert chuckled.

Sadie giggled. She thought Uncle Albert might well be to her liking. Kevin tugged open the door and they slid on to the back seat. They sank into the middle of it. The springs had gone a long time ago.

"You'll need to tie up the handle, Kevin," said Uncle Albert. "The catch is busted. I wouldn't be wanting you to fall out on a corner."

Kevin tied up the handle with the piece of string dangling from it, and settled back with his arm round Sadie.

"Right, we're off!" Uncle Albert pulled the starter. Nothing happened. He cursed, tried again.

"Looks like you'll need a push." Kevin untied the string and climbed out. He went round to the back of the car and pushed. They moved off by inches, gradually gathering a little more speed, and then with a splutter the car sprang to life again.

Uncle Albert slackened speed so that Kevin could catch them up. He got into the car panting.

"We'll be all right now," said Uncle Albert. "Once it gets going there's nothing to worry about." They chugged along slowly, being overtaken by anything else that was on the road. "There's life in the ould thing yet, Kevin. I always get there in the end."

"Been in Bangor, Uncle Albert?"

"I was seeing a man about a greyhound. Fine beast. I was tempted. But the missus'd have given me hell if I'd brought it back."

Kevin laughed, imagining the torrent of words Uncle Albert's wife would have poured out if he had returned with a dog.

"Haven't seen you before, have I, Sadie?" Uncle Albert half turned to have another look at Sadie. The car swerved slightly.

"Keep your eyes on the road, for dear sake, Uncle Albert. You nearly had us in the ditch."

"Have you been keeping her hidden, Kevin? You're a right lad! Where do you live then, Sadie?"

"Not far from Kevin," said Sadie, smiling to herself in the darkness.

"Funny I've never seen you before. I'd have remembered a girl like you if I had. You know how to pick them, Kevin."

"Don't listen to him, Sadie," said Kevin. "He's full of smooth talk."

They exchanged a few bits of banter. Sadie was enjoying herself. She liked the unexpected, missing the last bus, getting a lift in a funny old car. Tommy led such a dull, predictable life, going for walks with Linda, taking her to the cinema. They had the odd tiff but even they were dull and predictable: Linda would go off in the sulks and come out of them when she saw that she might be on the verge of losing Tommy.

Kevin sniffed. "You don't smell burning rubber, do you?"

"Burning rubber?" said Uncle Albert. "You're imagining things. Sure anyway there's always a bit of a smell in this ould car. What else could you expect with the age she is?"

"It's just as well they don't have those Ministry of Transport tests over here the way they do in England. You'd never get it through."

"Tests!" scoffed Uncle Albert. "I wouldn't have anything to do with them. Never sat an exam in my life. Always mitched on the days they had them. Not like your da, Kev. He was a serious scholar."

It hadn't got him very far, thought Kevin, working on a building site, but then he had had to leave school to help support his family. Just as he had had to do. He and his father were both eldest sons.

Sadie sniffed. She too fancied she could smell something burning but perhaps Uncle Albert was right: it was just part of the car. He must know it better than they did.

They came to a road junction where they had to stop. As soon as the car stopped the engine gave up too. Uncle Albert shook his head; Kevin untied the string and got out again.

"It's all right, Sadie," said Uncle Albert. "Another push and we'll be away."

But Kevin opened the door and said urgently, "There's smoke coming out of the bonnet."

Uncle Albert and Sadie jumped out quickly. Kevin lifted the bonnet and a cloud of steam gushed up into the air.

"Bless us!" said Uncle Albert, scratching his head. "What the devil's the matter with that then?"

"When did you last put water in?" asked Kevin.

"Only yesterday."

"Looks like your thermostat might be away."

Uncle Albert rested his hands on his hips and shook his head. He was not a member of any motoring organisation, naturally not, and he had not enough money on him to seek help at a garage. He had a friend who would be able to come out from Belfast the next day and take a look at it for him. Uncle Albert always had friends who could fix things but in the meantime they would have to abandon it. It grieved him to have to leave it lying on the road so far from home. They pushed it over to the side and back a little way from the junction.

"It won't blow up, will it?" asked Sadie.

"No, no." Kevin took a cloth, wrapped it round his hand and unscrewed the cap to let the rest of the steam escape. "It'll stop in a minute." When it did, he put down the lid of the bonnet.

"I hope no one siphons off me petrol," said Uncle Albert.

"I don't think you need worry too much about that."

"Or takes off me tyres. They're up to all sorts of tricks these days."

The tyres were so smooth they were on the verge of being dangerous, but Kevin did not point that out to his uncle. He wondered that the police did not pick him up more often for being in possession of an unroadworthy vehicle but then the police had plenty of other things to worry about.

"Looks like we'll have to walk," said Kevin.

Sadie walked between them, her arms linked through theirs. The sky had cleared and the moon rode high above them lighting the way. It was a fine night for a walk, Uncle Albert observed; he had walked home often enough before. And no doubt it would not be the last time, Kevin added. Uncle Albert broke into song, and Kevin and Sadie joined in.

After they had gone a mile or two they saw the lights ahead of a parked truck.

"Looks like an army check point," said Kevin.

When they drew near they saw two soldiers standing in front

59

of the truck, rifles held loosely in their hands. The walkers stopped in front of them.

"Where are you going?" asked one of the soldiers.

"Belfast," said Uncle Albert. "Me car broke down a bit back there on the road." He launched into a description of the expiring of the car until he was cut off by the soldier.

"And where have you been?"

"Bangor. I went to see a man about a greyhound."

"O.K. then, on you go."

"Trouble, son?"

"Army car blown up on one of the side roads," said the soldier shortly. "Landmine."

Uncle Albert tutted. "Nobody hurt I hope?"

"The driver was killed."

Sadie, Kevin and Uncle Albert walked on in silence for a way. And then Uncle Albert said, "Well, if they will come over here they have to expect trouble."

"But—" began Sadie, and then stopped as Kevin dug her in the ribs. She knew he was right: there was no point in arguing with Uncle Albert.

"It's not that I'm for people getting killed," said Uncle Albert. "And some of them soldiers are just boys." He sighed. "I don't know why we can't get a bit of peace."

They did not sing any more. They walked more briskly, eating up the miles, until they saw the lights of Belfast ahead. They tramped through the sleeping suburbs, their feet ringing out in the quietness. After the suburbs came the rows and rows of streets of little red-brick terraced houses, running parallel, each one almost identical. They walked closer together, their eyes swifting from side to side watching for signs of trouble.

"Wee bit of an argument up ahead," said Uncle Albert.

The army and a number of dark-clothed men were having a running battle with stones and rubber bullets. Without another word the three walkers turned off to the right and made a detour to avoid the area. They passed a burning shop. A few people stood in the street watching the flames as if they were mesmerised. Sadie shivered and held on tighter to the arms of the two men.

A church clock chimed three, and for the first time Sadie thought of her mother and father. She had forgotten them completely.

"We'll leave Sadie home first, will we, Kevin?" suggested Uncle Albert.

"No, no," said Kevin hastily. "I'll leave her home. You'd better get on back to your own house. Aunt Patsy'll be wondering where you are."

"Sure she knows better than to worry about me. But if that's the way you want it! You're only young once, eh Kevin?" Uncle Albert chuckled and took his arm from Sadie's. "Goodnight then, Sadie. It's been nice to meet you."

"You too, Mr. McCoy."

"Kevin must bring you up to meet the wife one of these days."

"That would be nice," said Sadie, knowing that Kevin would never be able to take her to his Uncle Albert's house.

"And the next time I give you a lift I'll see to it that the ould car doesn't let us down again."

Uncle Albert left them. Sadie and Kevin waited until he had gone from sight so that he would not see which direction they were taking.

"I liked your Uncle Albert," said Sadie.

"He's a good-natured soul. But he's a terrible husband."

"I could imagine that!"

They turned along the main road which led to Sadie's street. She drew in her breath.

"Kevin, there's three men coming." He looked and saw them too. They were still a good way off. "Don't you think you should go?" said Sadie.

"And leave you alone?"

"I'll be all right."

"No." He held her arm more firmly. "They look like a posse of vigilantes," he said jokingly.

The men were walking with a firm even tread as if they were out on patrol. As they drew nearer, Sadie felt certain that she was going to recognise them. Their outlines were familiar, their heights correct.

"It's them," she murmured. "I might have known it. Go on, go, please, Kevin," she said urgently.

But he stayed beside her. They met the men in the middle of the street. They stopped, with a few yards of pavement between them. Then Mr. Jackson, Mr. Mullet and Tommy advanced to confront Sadie and Kevin.

Chapter Nine

"Come here, Sadie," said Mr. Jackson, making a space for her between himself and Tommy.

Sadie stayed where she was, her arm resting against Kevin's.

"I'm sorry if you've been worried about Sadie," said Kevin, "but we went to Bangor and missed the last bus—"

"And then we got a lift from Kevin's Uncle Albert and his car broke down," carried on Sadie.

"I told you there'd be some quite simple reason for it, Da," said Tommy. He sounded awkward and embarrassed.

"Simple?" said Mr. Jackson.

"We've been searching the district for you for hours, Sadie," said Mr. Mullet. "The whole street's right upset and our Linda's near up the wall."

"Well, she'll just need to get down off it again," said Sadie.

"Boys, the cheek of it!" said Mr. Mullet softly. He was beginning to think his wife had been right all these years: Sadie Jackson was a bad influence and would come to no good in the end. It was only his friendship for Jim Jackson that had made them spend these last two hours scouring the streets. He would rather have been at home in his bed so that he would be up in good time for church in the morning. They had even gone to the edge of the Catholic quarter but had not dared to venture into it. There had been trouble over there. They had seen flames shooting up into the sky and the sound of shouting and then armoured cars had rumbled past. After that they had retreated.

"Come here, Sadie," her father repeated again. "I want no more of your nonsense. We've been up the walls tonight. Your mother'll need to go to the doctor for more pills."

"Sure she's always at the doctor for pills anyway."

Mr. Jackson lunged forward to catch hold of his daughter. She side-stepped. Tommy stirred uneasily wishing they could all go home and leave it at that. The more his father upbraided Sadie the more devilish she would become. His father *must* know that. He would only push her further into Kevin McCoy's arms.

"It's all right," said Sadie. "I'm coming home now anyway but I'm not going to be marched up the street as if I was being taken to the jail."

"The jail would be too good for you," said Mr. Mullet.

Mr. Jackson glared at Mr. Mullet. There was no call for a friend to make a remark like that about your daughter. There were a few remarks he could make about Linda if he chose to.

"Well, Jim, there's times a man must speak his mind," said Mr. Mullet. "We've nearly been round the bend this last two hours thinking of all the things that might have happened to her."

"Did you think the Micks had got hold of me and tarred and feathered me?" giggled Sadie.

"Careful," said Kevin softly, squeezing her arm.

"Let's go home to bed," said Tommy. "We've found Sadie and that's the main thing."

"That's not the main thing at all," said Mr. Jackson.

" 'Deed you're right, Jim." Mr. Mullet shook his head. "I agree. If it was our Linda—"

"I'm going home," said Tommy firmly. "Are you coming, Sadie?"

"Yes."

"That's right, you two go on home," said their father. "Mr. Mullet and I have some unfinished business with this fella here."

Tommy took a step over to his father. "Now look, Da, you're not going to start fighting."

"If you want to go home to your bed away you go. You don't seem to care who your sister's roaming about with till all hours of the night, but I do!" Mr. Jackson pushed his son away. His temper was up. It seldom rose, but when it did it did not subside easily.

Mr. Mullet stepped forward. He would stand by his Brother. In the Lodge they were all Brethren. And confronted by a Roman Catholic no good Orangeman would turn tail and run. He wondered if Tommy would be a good choice for Linda after all.

Sadie started to laugh. "What do you think you're going to fight Kevin for? He didn't force me to go with him. I went because I wanted to. He doesn't carry on any white slave traffic."

"White slave traffic?" said Mr. Mullet. "What kind of traffic is that?"

"Skip it," said Sadie. "And skip the fighting too. Because if you don't Kevin'll make mincemeat of the two of you with no bother at all."

"I'm not wanting any fighting either, Mr. Jackson," said Kevin.

"So you're a coward as well, eh?" said Mr. Mullet. "That doesn't surprise me. Any Mick who'd go sneaking off with a decent young Protestant girl behind her parents' back is sure to be yellow in the middle."

Now Kevin's temper soared. Sadie knew how high it could go. She tried to catch his arm but he had left her in a flash and was holding Mr. Mullet by the shoulders. He towered over Mr. Mullet by about four inches.

"If you were my own age I'd bash you for that!" Kevin

shouted. "But I don't pick on old men and stupid eejits for I like the odds to be even." He released Mr. Mullet.

"Old man? I'm not an old man. I was only forty-five last month."

Tommy rolled his eyes upward. "For heavens sake, let's go home. Ma'll be taking even more pills if we don't."

"I'm not going home till I sort this brat out," said Mr. Jackson, "And you needn't think it. By the time I'm done with him he'll not come near my daughter again. Right, Bill?"

Mr. Mullet moved forward less enthusiastically now. He was beginning to think Tommy might be right. It might be better to go home. Mr. Jackson advanced slowly towards Kevin. Suddenly Sadie jumped between them.

"If you want to fight him you'll have to take me on first."

"Sadie, I don't need you to fight my battles." Kevin tried to put her aside but she resisted.

If this went on any longer, thought Tommy, everybody would be fighting everyone else. He looked along the street. There were another two men coming. They must break the gathering up quickly before the other two arrived or there could be a real blood bath. And the blood would be Kevin's.

"Kevin," he said, "I think you should get on home. I know you don't want to fight my father."

"Course not."

"And I'm taking Sadie home. Now!"

Tommy jerked his head towards the end of the street. Both Sadie and Kevin noticed and got the message. Neither Mr. Jackson nor Mr. Mullet had seen that reinforcements were at hand.

"You're right, Tommy," said Sadie. "It's time we called it a day. Good-night, Kevin."

Kevin hesitated a moment.

"Good-night, Kevin," she said again, her eyes on the approaching men.

Kevin said good-night to Sadie and Tommy, then walked quickly off in the opposite direction. Tommy held back his father. Mr. Mullet required no restraining; his feet were already turning homewards.

Kevin zigzagged through the streets towards his own area. He had not wanted to leave in a way. His old instinct of wanting to fight it out had been there very strongly, but he knew it would have been stupid. He didn't want to fight Sadie's father and brother. Tommy would not have fought him anyway. They had no reason to fight one another.

He looked up and saw a glow in the sky. A fire. There was noise ahead too: the sound of rioting. He skirted the barbed-wire barricades. Two policemen asked him where he was going. Home, he said.

"Been trouble?" he asked.

"Plenty. Still is. Doyle's pub was burnt out."

Kevin moved on, tired now after the long day at the seaside and the walk. He walked close to the houses. The streets were astir with soldiers trying to clear up the last of the rioters. They were still fighting it out in isolated pockets. Kevin skirted these, taking several detours to get to his own street. The smell of burning was in the air.

A burst of machine gun fire sent him sprawling full length on the pavement. He lay with his face pressed against the cold ground, his heart racing. He looked sideways. Another burst. He put his arms round his head. He was not the target but the need to protect himself was instinctive. A vehicle roared past and stopped. Kevin eased himself on to his elbow. More armoured trucks, soldiers, police, gathered quickly. On the opposite pavement lay the victim of the attack.

The man was a civilian and he was dead.

Two policemen came to Kevin. Had he seen anything? He shook his head. Nothing, he told them, he had seen nothing, he had only heard the gunfire.

"Away off home then."

The policemen probably did not believe him, knowing full well that it would have been more than his life was worth to give away any information. He picked himself up and resumed his journey.

He broke into a trot when he reached the end of his street. He wanted to go to bed and sleep and shut out the sound of gunfire and shouting and the sight of men slumped on pavements.

"Hey there, Kevin!"

He halted. It was Brian Rafferty's voice.

Brian caught up with him. "Boys, they're getting a run for their money tonight all right!" He was grinning.

Kevin walked on. Brian fell into step beside him.

"Where've you been all day?"

"Bangor."

"You missed it all here. Doyle's pub got burnt down by the Prods. The cheek of them! They're going to pay for this. They'd burn us out to the last man if we let them."

"We do a bit of burning ourselves," said Kevin wearily.

Brian seized him by the shoulder and spun him round so that they stood face to face. "I don't like the sound of that talk."

"What good does burning things do? I'm sick of fires."

"So you take yourself off to Bangor for the day?"

"Why not? It's no crime."

"Could be. Depends on who you were with."

"What do you want to say?" Kevin shoved Brian's hand off his shoulder.

"I met your Uncle Albert on the way home. He was telling me you were with a blonde girl by the name of Sadie."

"So what?"

"I remember a girl called Sadie. Few years back."

"Mind your own business!" Kevin spoke fiercely.

"I don't know that it might not be my business, if it's the same Sadie I'm thinking of."

"You won't tell me what to do, Brian Rafferty."

"No?" Brian smiled and leaned back against the wall of a house.

68

"No." said Kevin and left him.

A few yards and he was home. He shut the door thankfully behind him, tiptoed upstairs in his stockinged feet and fell asleep on the bed fully clothed.

He wakened to the sound of church bells and Brede prodding him in the ribs.

"What time did you come in last night?"

"Haven't a clue." He yawned and stretched.

There was a smell of bacon in the house.

"Get up," said Brede, "or you'll be late for mass."

He washed, changed his clothes, went down to the kitchen.

The rest of the family had eaten. His mother was fussing about, washing faces and combing hair. All the children wore their best clothes. It was the only time in the week when they were all clean and tidy at the same time.

Kevin took his breakfast from the frying pan and sat down to eat.

His father began to question him. Where had he been last night? Had he been in any trouble? What time did he come in? All the usual questions. Kevin answered with a few words, telling nothing. Brede eyed him uneasily as she dried the last of the dishes.

They set off for church, the smaller children running in front playing tag, his mother and father walking slowly behind since his mother now walked with difficulty. Brede carried the youngest child over her shoulder with Kevin beside her.

When mass was over, the congregation loitered a while outside the church. The talk was all of the fire in Doyle's pub. Indignation was running high.

"You'd think it was something new!" said Kevin to Brede.

"I'm sick of death and burning," she said.

Brede sighed, shifting the baby higher on her shoulder. They walked home ahead of the others. Half way along their street they were overtaken by Kate. She was breathless.

"I've been calling you," she said.

"We didn't hear," said Brede. The baby cried and she joggled him up and down.

Kate eyed Kevin. "I was wondering what you were doing this afternoon. I thought we might all go for a picnic or something. What do you say?"

"I'm busy," said Kevin, and he carried on up the street, leaving the two girls together.

"What's up with him?" Kate pouted.

"Maybe—" Brede hesitated. "Maybe you shouldn't chase him as much, Kate. Boys don't like to be run after."

"How dare you, Brede McCoy!" Kate tossed her head. "I've never run after a boy in my life."

"I was just trying to be helpful." The baby began to cry again. "I'll need to get him home for his bottle," said Brede.

Kate went back down the street and on the way met Brian Rafferty.

As Brede went inside her house she looked back and saw that Brian and Kate had their heads together and were deep in conversation.

After lunch, Kevin left the house and walked to Cave Hill. He spent the afternoon up there alone, lying in the sunshine, drifting into sleep from time to time.

In the early evening he came down to the city again on to the tow path of the River Lagan, where he had arranged to meet Sadie. She arrived a few minutes after he did. He saw her coming, walking with a long smooth stride, her fair hair blowing back in the breeze. He liked the look of her walking towards him with a smile on her face. He smiled too.

He caught both her hands in his.

"I was wondering if you'd come," he said.

"You didn't really. You knew I would."

"Yes."

They wandered along the path, their arms around one another's waists. They passed other young couples, also walking arms entwined, or hand in hand. Sometimes, when they passed another couple, they all four smiled at each other, as if they were sharing a secret.

"Does your mother know you're out?" asked Kevin, and Sadie laughed.

"I'm always out. I hate being stuck in the house."

"Me too."

"Houses are too small," said Sadie. "I'd like to live in a tent in a field."

"What about a caravan?"

"We could be tinkers," said Sadie. "I'd quite fancy the life. Trotting along the roads with nobody to bother you. Are you any good with a horse?"

"A horse? Sure I can handle them as smooth as silk." Kevin laughed. "As long as they're fifty years old and ready to be pensioned off."

They stayed by the river until the last light faded from the sky and the air was cool.

"It's been a lovely evening," sighed Sadie.

"When can I see you again, Sadie?"

"When would you like to?"

"Tomorrow?"

She nodded.

"Same place?"

"Same place."

They turned homewards. They decided they would part before they came near their own areas. They agreed that it was only a nuisance to have encounters like last night's.

Several streets away from Sadie's they stopped and sought refuge from the night wind in a shop doorway. Sadie said that she ought to be getting home so that she didn't get another row for being late but Kevin kept hold of her hand. They stayed there talking for half an hour.

A clock nearby chimed midnight.

"Time passes quickly," said Sadie. "I'd really better go."

He kissed her. "See you tomorrow."

"Yes. Half seven." She lingered still.

"Only nineteen hours and a bit."

"Not long ..."

They kissed again and then she left him, looking back from the next corner to wave.

She thought about him all the way home. When she came in her mother raged at her for being late but she did not even answer back. She drifted up the stairs with a little smile on her face. Mrs. Jackson's eyes narrowed suspiciously.

"I didn't like the look in Sadie's eye," said Mrs. Jackson to her husband when they lay in bed in the room next to Sadie's. "She was supposed to be going out with some girls from her work but I've got my doubts. Jim, you don't think she would have been meeting that McCoy boy again do you? Jim!" She nudged him. But Mr. Jackson was asleep and when she stopped talking she heard him snoring.

Kevin walked home thinking of Sadie too. He liked the way her eyes danced and her mouth lifted in a mischievous smile. She was full of life and energy that seemed to match his. They matched. He smiled at the thought. In some ways it was ridiculous, but there it was. He whistled to himself.

He came round by the side of the scrapyard, quite unprepared for the attack. The three boys were upon him before he even had the chance to see their faces. But he knew who one was, for the laugh was familiar and the voice. "Traitor!" He fought back blindly, without a chance. He went down on to the ground, face downwards, his arms protectively over his head. He felt their feet, and that was all ...

Chapter Ten

Brede cleared up the mess of sand and water, put away a jig-saw, sorted out a jumble of toys. End of the day jobs. Not many children were left in the nursery now. Mothers had been coming in and out for the last half hour collecting their children. Brede kept an eye on the clock hoping that everyone would come on time and she would not be kept late. There were usually one or two mothers who rushed in at the last possible moment indignantly spilling out tales of delayed buses or being kept late at work.

"Anything wrong, Brede?" asked the matron.

Brede looked up, startled, from where she knelt on the floor amongst the toys.

"Are you all right, Brede?"

"Yes." Brede pushed a strand of hair from her eyes.

"You've looked very troubled all day. Are you sure? Anything wrong at home?"

"Well ..."

"Is it your mother? She must be getting near her time. Would you like to get away now? I'll finish off for you."

Brede thanked her, went up to the cloakroom and took off her overall. There would still be time for her to get across the town to the department store where Sadie worked.

She had to wait for a bus and when it came it seemed to travel like a snail out for a Sunday stroll. The shop would shut at six, she hoped, not before. She *must* catch Sadie before she left.

She alighted at the City Hall and ran through the crowds to the shop. At the enquiry desk she asked which department Sadie Jackson worked in.

"Hat department."

Hats were on the second floor. Brede did not wait for the lift; she ran up the stairs and arrived in the quiet hush of the hat department with a stitch in her side. There was no sign of Sadie. A middle-aged woman in a black dress was helping a customer try on a large yellow picture hat.

"Madam, it's absolutely perfect!" declared the saleswoman. "It shows off your face beautifully."

Madam did not seem so sure. She twisted this way and that, looking at herself in the mirror from every angle. Brede circled round the hat stands, unable to imagine Sadie in such a place.

"It really is your colour, madam." The saleswoman looked over her shoulder at Brede. She ran her eyes over Brede's rather shabby summer dress and scuffed sandals and obviously did not consider her to be much of a prospect for the sale of a picture hat. Brede blushed a little but stood her ground.

"I don't know . . ." The customer fingered her chin, and then suddenly made up her mind. She whipped off the hat. "No, I think I'll leave it for today, thank you."

"That's all right, madam," said the saleswoman, stiff-lipped.

She began to gather up the dozen or so hats that the customer had been trying on for the past half-hour.

Brede approached her nervously. "Excuse me . . ."

"I'm afraid we're about to close."

"It's not that. I don't want to buy a hat."

"I didn't think you did." The saleswoman bundled several hats into a drawer.

"I'm actually looking for Sadie Jackson."

74

"You won't find her here. She got the sack this morning," said the woman triumphantly.

Brede fled from the shop. How was she to see Sadie now? There was only one place where she knew she could find her.

She knew the name of Sadie's street, and that her house was the end one, with a mural of King Billy on its gable wall. Kevin had told her that. She had never been in the street herself before.

Brede advanced into the warren of Protestant streets with her heart beating. It was unlikely that anyone would recognise her, she knew that, but still she felt a tug of fear at her heart. The houses were very like her own, small, brick terraced, back-to-back, but the signs on the walls were different. LONG LIVE KING BILLY. KICK THE POPE. NO SURRENDER. When a child turned suddenly in front of her, she thought he was going to point his finger at her and shout, "She's a Mick, come and get her!" But he looked to the side of her and called to another boy further back. Brede passed him, face hot, lips dry. She went down one street, turned into another, looked at the name, could not find the right one. She would have to ask. On a corner stood a small shop with an open door. She went inside, picking her way between crates of lemonade and milk and bags of potatoes. There was only one customer, a woman with her hair in rollers and high-heeled shoes on her swollen feet. She was being served by a woman with an enormous bosom that rested on the counter.

They both eyed her, knowing at once that she was strange to the area. Brede swallowed.

"It's all right, Mrs. McConkey, you can serve this girl first. I'm in no hurry."

"As long as you're sure, Mrs. Mullet." Mrs. McConkey looked at Brede. "What can I get you then?"

"Bar of milk chocolate," said Brede quickly. She took the money from her purse. She had just enough to pay for it.

Mrs. McConkey shuffled over to the shelf, took down the

bar of chocolate and shuffled back to the counter again. It gave Mrs. Mullet plenty of time to examine Brede.

Brede passed over the money. As she moved towards the door she paused and asked for directions to Sadie's street.

"I live there," said Mrs. Mullet. "Hang on a minute and I'll walk you along. Just give me six eggs, Mrs. McConkey, and I'll pay you tomorrow."

Mrs. McConkey passed the eggs over reluctantly.

"Thanks a lot." Mrs. Mullet said to Brede, "Come on then and I'll show you the way. Are you looking for anyone in particular?"

"Well ... actually, the Jacksons' house."

Mrs. Mullet stopped on the pavement. "The Jacksons? Fancy that, they're old friends of mine. Their son Tommy's courting my Linda."

"That's nice." Brede moistened her lips, wishing that her throat was not as dry and her heart not thumping quite so loudly.

Mrs. Mullet tripped across the road on her spiky heels, Brede finding difficulty in walking slowly enough to stay with her.

"Is it far?" she asked.

"Just the next street."

The next street! Why couldn't the woman have said so and saved her all this waste of time? Of course she knew very well why.

"Don't come from round here, do you?"

"No."

"Known the Jacksons long?"

"No."

"Is it Sadie you're looking for?"

"Yes."

"Work with her, do you?"

Brede tipped her head, as if in assent. They passed a mural of King William astride his white horse, with REMEMBER 1690 written below. This must be the house.

Mrs. Mullet took her round the corner and rang the bell.

"Please don't bother," said Brede.

"No trouble." Mrs. Mullet pushed open the door and called out, "Anyone in? You've got a visitor."

It was Tommy who came to the door. He looked at Brede and then at Mrs. Mullet.

"I met Sadie's friend in the shop so I brought her round."

Tommy continued to stare at Brede.

"Who is it, Tommy?" Mrs. Jackson called from within.

"Friend of Sadie's," Tommy called back, pulling the door to behind him. "Thanks then, Mrs. Mullet," he said.

She was dismissed. She did not hurry across the street, and when she reached the opposite pavement her shoe came off and she had to spend considerable time putting it on.

"What is it, Brede?" Tommy spoke quietly, a frown creasing his brow.

"I haven't come to cause trouble," she said.

"I know that. Don't be daft. It's nice to see you."

"And you." She smiled. "But I came to see Sadie. I must. Is she in?"

Tommy nodded. "She's upstairs getting ready to go out. You've just caught her. I think she's going to meet Kevin but I don't know."

"She is. That's why I want to speak to her."

"Wait here. I'll get her."

Brede stood close to the house, aware that the Mullets' lace curtain was being held back and two pairs of eyes were watching her. Sadie came quickly.

"What's up, Brede?" she asked.

"Can we go somewhere? Somewhere we can talk."

Sadie pulled the door shut behind her and together they walked up the street.

"Your neighbours are watching," said Brede.

Sadie turned and waved at the Mullets' house. The lace curtain dropped. Brede laughed, forgetting her troubles for a moment.

"You haven't changed much, Sadie. I'm glad."

"It's great to see you, Brede. But I haven't got long. I'm meeting Kevin at half seven."

"That's what I've come to see you about."

Sadie sighed. "You're not going to try to talk me out of seeing him too, are you? I've had Tommy at me already. It's not that he's got anything against Kevin, you know that. But it's peace at any price for him!"

"Peace would be nice," said Brede.

"Sometimes the price is too high."

"Sometimes the price is high the other way too."

Sadie glanced at Brede and frowned. "We'll go to a little café further along the main street. No one'll bother us there."

The café was empty. Sadie bought two cups of coffee and they sat at the back of the shop, their chairs close together.

"You need a hot drink, Brede. You're dead pale looking."

Brede took a sip of coffee before she spoke. "We had a shock last night."

"Kevin?" asked Sadie swiftly.

"Yes. He was beaten up."

"Badly?"

"Quite. A lot of bruises, and a cut on his head and leg. He'd to get three stitches in his head."

"Oh, my goodness!" Sadie gulped, putting her hand to her mouth.

"Is he all right?"

"More or less. Mr. Kelly found him lying outside the scrapyard late last night. He was unconscious. Mr. Kelly called an ambulance and they took him to hospital."

"Is he there now?"

"They let him home this morning."

"Was it because of me, Brede? Was it?"

"Yes, I think so." Brede's voice was scarcely audible. Her eyes were unhappy.

"Who did it?"

"There were three of them. One was Brian Rafferty. He used to be Kevin's friend."

"Three of them! Cowards! If I got my hands on them!"

"They'd do the same to you."

Sadie finished her coffee with one gulp. "Did he ask you to come and tell me?"

"No. He doesn't know I'm here. He's going out to meet you, Sadie, I know it." Brede raised her eyes to Sadie's. "He'll not let you down. But I've come to ask you not to meet him."

"But that would mean I'd be letting him down," cried Sadie.

"But you don't want him to be beaten up again, do you?"

"No. But—"

"Then don't see him again. Please don't see him again," Brede pleaded.

"You mean not even tonight? Let him wait there and me not come ... He'd think I'd stood him up."

"Sadie, it might be best. He's too proud to try to see you again if you don't see him. I know it's hard but it would be easier for him if he thought you'd given in. After all, *he* was beaten up."

It was very quiet in the café. The proprietor had gone through to the back room. The sound of the traffic from the street was curiously distant and remote. Sadie looked into Brede's pleading, anxious eyes, eyes the same colour as her brother's, dark brown, flecked with lighter specks. "I know it's hard," Brede repeated. Sadie felt a lump in her throat like a boil that was threatening to burst at any moment.

"I don't know, Brede, I don't know..." I don't know anything at all, thought Sadie, I don't seem to know anything. I want to see Kevin and he wants to see me and all these people are trying to get between us. Everything in life had seemed straightforward before: there had been choices but she had never been afraid to choose, and to choose what she felt was right. What was right here: to give in to Brian Rafferty and his friends and Linda Mullet and her family and all the others, or to do what she wanted to do? It didn't seem much to ask, to want to walk by the river, to climb a hill with someone you liked.

"You don't want him to be hurt again, do you?" Brede was saying, cutting into her thoughts.

"Of course not."

"Then you won't see him?" Brede sat back.

"I'm not sure." Sadie lifted her head. "I can't promise, Brede. I have to think about it."

"Think carefully then." Brede stood up. She straightened her back, with her hand at the side of her hip, the way her mother did when she was tired. "There's times when it might be all right for a Catholic boy to be walking out with a Protestant girl, but now's not one of them. And in streets like these. There's enough blood, Sadie, without any more getting shed."

And with that, Brede left the café. Sadie stared at the sticky rims on the red formica-topped table. What Brede said was true. And Brede's motives were good. She liked Brede: that was why she had listened. If Linda Mullet had said the same things she would have walked out defiantly to meet Kevin McCoy. But now ... Now what?

She looked at the clock above the café counter. Ten minutes past seven. In twenty minutes time Kevin would be standing by the river waiting for her, trusting that she would come.

The café proprietor came back. "Another coffee?" he asked.

She shook her head. She got up, pushed back her chair, and walked out into the fresh air.

Chapter Eleven

Kevin walked stiffly along the path beside the river. His head throbbed, and from time to time he had to stop to rest. He carried his left arm in a sling; his shoulder had been badly bruised. At the hospital they had said it was lucky he was so strong and well-built. He had come out of it all remarkably well. But still he was shaken, and he had never felt before such weakness in his body. He would not be able to work for a week or two and he knew that Mr. Kelly would not be able to pay him when he wasn't working. Sickness benefit would not make up his pay. Another worry for his mother, who was full enough of worries already.

She had been worried when he had come out this evening. "You can't go out, Kevin," she had said, but he had told her he must. He could not let Sadie down, leave her standing waiting for him, wondering why he had not come. And he had no way of sending her a message, no one he could have asked to go to her house and explain. Brede might have been willing but he would not have asked her to take the risk for him.

A clock sounded the half hour. He limped the last few yards to the spot where they had arranged to meet. She was not there yet. He sighed with relief. He leaned against a tree and took a few deep breaths. He had made it, even though he had had to walk like an old man! He grinned to himself. It was cooler tonight that it had been the evening before, or perhaps it was just that he was feeling the cold. Rest in bed for a week, they had told him. Lie in bed for a week! It would be like lying in prison.

There were not so many people around tonight either. Of course it was Monday. Sundays brought out the young couples. One or two passed him, glancing at him as they passed. He knew he must be a fine looking sight for sore eyes: head bandaged, a black eye, arm in a sling.

He looked back along the path searching for any sign of Brian Rafferty in case he had been followed. But he was sure that he had not. He had sent out Gerald earlier to see what Rafferty was up to, and Gerald had come back to say he had seen Rafferty and his friends heading out towards another district. His family knew who had beaten him up but they also knew as he did, it was better not to tell the police. When they had questioned him at the hospital he had said that he had no idea who had jumped him. He would be jumped again if he had told: that was a certainty.

An elderly man came along with his dog. He was throwing a stick for the dog and when the dog brought it back his owner clapped him and said, "Good boy, Jack." They looked happy, the man and his dog. As he drew level with Kevin, the man stopped.

"Are you all right, son?" he asked, coming closer.

"Yes. Thanks."

"Are you sure? Do you want me to help you along the path?"

No, no, Kevin assured him, he was all right, he would not pass out. The dog stood panting beside them, the stick between his teeth, waiting to be praised.

"All right, Jack, all right," said the man.

The man's face swam out of focus as if it was drifting under water. Kevin blinked, took another deep breath and steadied himself against the tree. The man put his arms round him.

"You're not all right, are you? Come on, I'm going to take you home."

"No."

"Where do you live? I have a car just along the street."

Kevin shook his head. "Let me sit down," he said weakly.

He slid down to the ground and sat with his head resting against the bark of the tree. He felt a bit better now. He could see the man's face clearly again: very bright blue eyes, looking at him with concern, creased forehead, a neat little moustache. The man was crouching beside him, and the dog was still waiting patiently with the stick.

"I think you need a doctor."

"I'm just weak. I had an accident, you see, last night."

"I don't like leaving you here like this." The man shook his head.

"I'm waiting for someone. What time is it?"

The man looked at his watch. "Ten to eight."

"Ten to eight?"

"Is she late then?" The man smiled a little.

Kevin nodded.

"Maybe she won't come."

"She'll come."

"You sound pretty sure."

"Well, I know her."

"I should hope so."

Kevin tried to smile but the wound in his head hurt when he did. The man sat down beside him.

"I'll wait with you till she comes."

"No, don't bother. You don't need to."

"But if she doesn't come ..."

"She will."

"I tell you what. I'll walk the dog along the rest of the path and come back this way. If she's not here by then I'll take you home. All right?"

Kevin agreed. But Sadie would come. Unless of course her family was keeping her in the house ... It would take a lot to restrain Sadie. He knew she had dropped out of her bedroom window before now. He watched the man and his dog go out of sight. A clock chimed the hour.

She was not going to come. Of course she would come. She *must* come. She would not let him down. Why should she come? She was a pretty girl, she could find plenty of boys, Protestant boys, to take her out. Safe boys. But Sadie never played safe. Why should she want him? His head was confused. He put his hand to it.

If she did not come by the time the man returned then he would go. He was not capable of waiting any longer...

He heard the man's voice before he saw him. "Good boy, Jack!" And then the dog came running, the stick firmly in his jaw, to stop beside Kevin's feet.

Kevin looked up at the man.

"I think I should take you now, don't you?"

Kevin nodded, tried to rise, collapsed at the knees. The man put his hands under his armpits and helped him to his feet.

"Now lean on me and take it easy, and you'll be all right."

They moved slowly along the path. Kevin's legs felt like candles beneath him.

"Where do you live, boy?"

Kevin hesitated. He knew the man was a Protestant: one could always tell when you had been brought up to know the difference at a distance of fifty yards. The man might not want to bring his car into Kevin's street, past barricades and army patrols.

"I'm a Catholic," he said.

"And I'm not," said the man. "But if you think that means I'm going to drop you by the side of the river you've another think coming."

"But I live in a troubled area. You don't have to take me right into it."

"Well, we'll see about that when we get there," said the man cheerfully. He looked back at his dog and whistled to him. "What's your name, boy?"

"Kevin."

"Right, Kevin, a few more yards and we'll be there."

"Kevin! Kevin!" Sadie's voice reached them. It was loud, almost frantic.

Kevin stopped. She had come!

"She's come," he said.

Sadie was running, her feet flying along the path scarcely touching it, her hair streaming out behind her. They waited for her: the man, the dog and Kevin.

"Why, it's Sadie Jackson," said the man. "Fancy that!"

"Oh, Kevin!" she cried, when she reached them. Her breath came in loud gulps. She put her hand under her ribs.

Kevin smiled at her in spite of the throb in his head. He had known all along that she would come. He had had no cause to doubt her.

"I nearly missed you," she gasped.

"But you didn't, Sadie," said the man, "and that's the main thing."

Sadie turned to him. "It's—" she paused, "—Mr. Blake." She had almost called him Twinkle Blake. That had been his nickname at school. Twinkle, because of his eyes.

"Haven't seen you since you left school. But I recognised you at once." He chuckled. "You could always run fast."

"Do you know one another then?" asked Kevin.

"I taught her at school. Come on, Sadie, let's get this boy into the car. He's going to keel over in a minute."

Between them they supported Kevin to the car and eased him on to the front seat. Blood was seeping through the bandage on his head now. Sadie got into the back of the car with the dog.

"Are you going home with Kevin?" asked Mr. Blake, then he added, "But you can't very well, can you?"

"No."

"Could you drop us off somewhere?" asked Kevin.

"We need to go some place quiet to talk," said Sadie.

"O.K.," said Mr. Blake. "I know just the place."

Kevin slumped back in his seat, eyes closed. Sadie and Mr. Blake talked of old pupils and teachers at school exchanging pieces of news, and he told her that he had retired the previous summer. He was driving them out to one of the suburbs. The houses changed from terraced to small semi-detached with no gardens, and then to slightly larger ones with gardens and hedges and gates.

Mr. Blake turned off the main road and stopped in a quiet street.

"This is my house," he said, indicating one with a white gate and a laburnum tree overhanging the pavement. "You can come in and sit in peace."

"Smashing!" said Sadie.

They helped Kevin indoors and laid him on the settee in the sitting room. It was a comfortable, tidy room, with family photographs on the mantelpiece and piano.

"I'm a widower," said Mr. Blake. "My wife died two years ago and my family's grown up."

"So you live alone?" said Sadie.

"Yes. Sit down, Sadie, I'm going to make you both a cup of coffee and then I'm going to ring my doctor and ask if he'd mind having a look at Kevin's head. He's an old friend of mine and he'll oblige me, I'm sure."

Kevin tried to protest but found he was too tired. Sadie sat on the edge of the settee and took hold of Kevin's hand.

"I'm sorry I was late, Kevin. You see, Brede came to see me—"

"Brede?"

"She told me what had happened."

"She asked you not to come, didn't she?"

"Yes. For your sake. She was worried about you and I didn't know what to do. But I couldn't bear the thought of you waiting."

"I'm glad you couldn't." His hand tightened round hers.

Mr. Blake came in carrying a tray. Sadie jumped up to help him.

"The coffee won't be up to much, I'm afraid," he said. "I'm not very handy in the kitchen. Still, I do my best. I've got hold of the doctor and he's on his way."

As Kevin drank the coffee, colour returned to his cheeks. His face, normally so brown and healthy, looked waxy and yellow. When the doctor arrived, Sadie and Mr. Blake retired to the kitchen to wash up the dishes.

"I'll wash," said Sadie.

"And I'll dry," said Mr. Blake. He stood with the tea towel in his hand waiting for her to start. "I told the doctor a little bit of what had happened so that he wouldn't ask Kevin too many questions. Goodness knows, he must be sick of questions! Poor lad. But he's a brave one, Sadie, he wouldn't give in. He was sitting there waiting for you and all the time he was on the verge of fainting. You're lucky to have such a nice boy."

"I know." Sadie's face was serious. "But it's not easy."

The doctor joined them in the kitchen. He washed his hands at the sink. "Nothing serious," he said. "At least no more than it was before. But the stitches hadn't burst. The wound was bleeding, that was all. I've changed the dressing and made him more comfortable. Of course he should never have been out walking about at all."

"I'll see he gets home safely," promised Mr. Blake.

"Good."

The doctor went off swinging his black bag.

"You go on through and talk to Kevin now, Sadie," said Mr. Blake. "And in a wee while I'll run him home. He needs to get to his bed soon."

Sadie found Kevin sitting up with his back against a cushion. He looked much better. He even grinned at her, and then winced. "Ouch!"

"Serves you right," said Sadie. "No grinning for you for a while!" She smiled at him.

"Come and sit beside me and tell me something nice." He patted the edge of the settee.

She sat down. "I want to talk to you but I don't know if it's going to be nice. You see, I decided I'd come to see you tonight, but I decided it would have to be the last time."

Chapter Twelve

"The last time," repeated Kevin.

"It's not because I don't want to see you," said Sadie. "You know I do."

"So you're going to give in to them?" Kevin's voice had an edge of bitterness.

"It's not a case of giving in."

"What is it then?" he demanded.

"I don't want you to get hurt again," she said simply. "That's all."

They were quiet for a moment before Kevin spoke. "I'm sorry, I didn't mean to sound angry with you, Sadie. It's just that I hate the idea of Brian Rafferty telling me what to do."

"It's not just Brian Rafferty, is it? If it wasn't him it would be somebody else. Every time I left you I'd be wondering if you were going to be beaten up on the way home."

"They needn't know, we could meet in secret."

"Where?"

Kevin sighed. He closed his eyes.

Mr. Blake knocked before he entered. He put his head round the door and looked at them. Then he came in and shut the door. He sat down.

"What's the matter? The two of you don't look very happy."

"We're not," said Kevin. "Sadie thinks we'll have to give up seeing one another."

Mr. Blake shook his head. He reached out to a pipe rack, took down a pipe and began to fill it with tobacco. "It's a pity that. Since you seem so fond of one another. But I know it must be difficult."

Sadie felt herself blush. Yes, it was true: she was fond of Kevin; that was why she could not bear to have him hurt.

"It is difficult," she said. "Even to meet."

Kevin had closed his eyes again. His face looked pale and exhausted.

"I think we'll have to get that boy home," said Mr. Blake.

They helped him back into the car. Sadie sat in the back as before.

"You've got to let me off outside my neighbourhood," Kevin insisted. "I'll manage the last bit alone."

"All right," said Mr. Blake. "I'm not happy at letting you walk but there's no point in causing any more trouble." He stopped the car in a side street. "Will you make it from here?" Kevin nodded. He put his hand on the handle of the door and looked round at Sadie. Was this to be the last time they would see one another?

"I tell you what," said Mr. Blake. "Would the two of you like to come round to my house for supper one evening?"

"We'd love to, wouldn't we, Kevin?"

"Yes," said Kevin.

"Shall we say Friday?" suggested Mr. Blake. "That'll give Kevin a few days to be going about again."

"See you Friday then," said Kevin.

He opened the door. They watched him as he walked up the street. He was limping badly but walking fairly steadily. At the corner he turned to wave, then was gone. Sadie moved over on to the front seat beside Mr. Blake.

"I hope he'll be all right," she said.

"Don't worry. He'll make it. He looks a tough one."

Mr. Blake drove Sadie home. They passed several armoured

cars heading in the opposite direction.

"These are bad times, Sadie," sighed Mr. Blake. "Especially for a Protestant girl to be keeping company with a Catholic boy."

"I know," she said soberly. "Do you think I'm mad, Mr. Blake?"

"Yes," he said. "And I should probably give you good advice and tell you to give it up. You can't always walk with the crowd, especially if you don't like the way they're walking. But I like you for it. It takes a bit of courage. You were never lacking in that."

Sadie felt herself blush again. She was not one who blushed easily but that was twice Mr. Blake had made her blush in a few hours. He was a very open and honest man, she remembered that from schooldays. He always said what it was in his mind to say.

He stopped outside her house. She opened the car door.

"Good night, Mr. Blake. And thanks for everything. I think you're super."

His blue eyes twinkled. "A few years back you were probably saying quite the opposite, eh?"

"I'm changing in my old age. See you. Thanks again."

She stood on the pavement, waving until he was out of sight. She was still shaking her head with admiration when Tommy came out of the front door.

"Who was that brought you home?"

"Twinkle Blake. Do you remember him? The geography teacher."

Tommy frowned. "What were you doing with him?"

Sadie told him about Kevin meeting him on the Lagan path. Tommy was impressed by Mr. Blake's kindness but troubled that Sadie was going to see Kevin again.

"Where'll it all end?" he wanted to know.

"I can't think about that," said Sadie. Beginnings were more interesting. "But do you know what happened to me this morning?"

"No, but I soon will."

"The old bitch in the hat department said to me, 'I hear you're keeping company with a Mick'."

"And what did you say?" asked Tommy, resigned to hearing the worst.

"I told her to go to hell and she gave me the sack."

"Will you never learn to keep your mouth shut?"

"Why should I? She opened hers first."

"What'll Ma say when she hears you're out of work?"

"I'm not going to tell her till I get another job."

A loud bang nearby made them jump. It had sounded like the crack of an explosion. Almost at once other noises followed the first one: screaming, shouting, commotion. It was coming from the next street.

They ran round the corner. Mrs. McConkey's shop was going up in flames.

A number of people had gathered in the street already. Most of them were running around shouting. Mr. Mullet was there waving his arms.

"Sadie, go quick and get a policeman," said Tommy.

Sadie went. One did not have to go far without encountering a policeman or soldier. She found two policemen in the main street. They had heard the explosion and were coming to investigate.

Within several minutes the narrow street was filled with fire engines, police cars and people. The police ordered the spectators out of the street and began to evacuate the families in the houses near Mrs. McConkey's shop.

The Jacksons and the Mullets retreated round the corner. They stood in front of the Jacksons' house to await news. Fresh rumours came with every person who passed. The shop had been blown up by gelignite, a petrol bomb, three petrol bombs ... Four masked men had been seen in the street. Mrs. McConkey was dead. Mrs. McConkey was rushed to hospital. Mrs. McConkey had not been found.

"God help us all," said Mrs. Jackson. "It could be our turn next."

Sadie thought of Mr. Blake in his nice quiet house. She wished she could get away from this street. She used to enjoy it, the life and movement, and always someone standing in a doorway ready to pass the time of day.

"What about a cup of tea?" she asked.

Her mother turned to her in surprise. "What's up with you? Offering to make tea?"

Sadie shrugged. "I'll go in and put the kettle on."

"Away and help her, Linda," said Mrs. Mullet, but Linda did not want to miss anything in the street.

"It's all right," said Sadie, who did not want Linda's company anyway. She wanted to be alone to think.

She set the kettle on the gas and took down the cups from their hooks. The kitchen was spotlessly clean and tidy. Her mother was a good housewife. "You could eat off the floor," she was fond of saying proudly, but Sadie always asked who would want to eat off the floor.

After a few minutes Tommy joined her. "It seems they've got Mrs. McConkey out. But she's badly burned."

"Poor Mrs. McConkey," sighed Sadie.

They would never again lean on her counter amongst the trays of sweets and rows of newspapers and comics. A part of their childhood had gone.

"The tea's ready," said Sadie. "Will you call them in?"

The two families sat down in the kitchen together.

"The firemen are still at it," said Mr. Jackson. "The shop's a goner, that's for sure."

"Let's hope Mrs. McConkey's not," said Mrs. Jackson.

"And to think I was in there just a few hours ago having a a yarn with her," sniffed Mrs. Mullet. She lifted her head thoughtfully. "There was a girl came in when I was there. A stranger."

"Have a biscuit, Mrs. Mullet," said Sadie quickly, thrusting the plate under Mrs. Mullet's nose.

Mrs. Mullet took a biscuit absentmindedly. "Yes, she came here afterwards."

"She had nothing to do with it," said Tommy shortly.

"It was Kevin McCoy's sister, wasn't it?" said Linda. "I saw her from the window."

"Kevin McCoy's sister?" said Mr. Jackson.

"What if it was?" Sadie got up, took her cup and saucer to the sink and washed them. "You're not trying to say that she was in the shop planting a stick of gelignite?"

"How do we know what she was in here for?" demanded Mrs. Mullet.

"Well, what *was* she here for?" asked Mrs. Jackson. "It's the first I knew of her being here at all."

"There's a lot going on without you knowing, Mrs. Jackson, I'm thinking," said Mrs. Mullet.

"Go on, then, Sadie," said Linda, planting her elbows on the table, "tell us what she was here for."

"Why should I? It was private, between us."

"Maybe that's what you think," said Linda. "Maybe she was sent to spy out the lie of the land."

"Don't be so stupid!" Tommy turned on Linda.

Mr. Mullet got to his feet. "Don't you dare speak to our Linda like that! Come on, Linda, Jessie, we're going home. It seems that Tommy and Sadie aren't fussy about who they keep company with, but I'm fussy about my daughter's company."

The Mullets ushered their daughter out before she could get a chance to protest.

"Good riddance to bad rubbish!" declared Sadie.

"That'll do, Sadie," said her mother. "There's no need to cause any more trouble. We've enough as it is."

"But the cheek of them suggesting Brede McCoy was coming round here to help blow up Mrs. McConkey!"

"And what was Brede McCoy doing round here?"

"I told you before: it was private."

"That's not a good enough answer."

"It'll have to do," said Sadie. She left the kitchen and went up to bed.

In the morning her mother was tight-lipped and silent. Sadie ate her breakfast and left the house at the usual time. She went round to the next street. On the corner was a blackened shell that had once been a shop. The adjoining house was slightly damaged and there were signs of a hasty removal.

As she stood on the pavement she saw Steve coming along on his way to work. She was about to move away when he called her.

"Bad bit of work that, eh?" She agreed, and he said, "They'll not get away with it."

"What's the point in going on? They'll just come back again. It could go on forever."

"You're wrong! There's more of us. Anyway, Sadie Jackson, you've changed your tune a bit these last few years."

"There's some never sing anything but the one note all their lives!"

She walked off before he had the chance to reply. She liked to have the last word, she knew it full well, but who better to have it with than someone like Steve?

Linda was at the bus stop. They ignored one another in the queue but when they got on the bus Linda came and sat beside her.

"I didn't really mean what I said last night," said Linda.

"Why say it then?" snapped Sadie. She looked out of the window the rest of the way into town. She was not going to give Linda Mullet any satisfaction. Brede McCoy was worth ten of her. Linda chattered on regardless.

Sadie tried to lose her at the City Hall but Linda was persistent. She kept in step with Sadie all the way along the street to the shop where Sadie worked. Had worked. She was going to have to go inside now, pretend that she still did work there. Linda was a typist in an office a few yards further on.

"Will I see you at lunch time?" asked Linda.

"I'm busy for lunch."

Sadie left her abruptly and went in through the side entrance for employees. She met the head of the hat department inside the door.

"What do you think you're doing here?"

"Just taking a last nostalgic look," said Sadie and walked out again. She saw the rear view of Linda disappearing into the crowd.

Sadie walked back along to the City Hall. She supposed she should go to the Labour Exchange and try to get a job but they would probably offer her another job in a shop and she felt she could not face that.

In front of the City Hall the news vendors were selling the morning papers. She saw their billboards. SHOP BURNED DOWN. WOMAN DEAD.

So Mrs. McConkey was dead. Sadie felt a wave of sickness rise in her throat. Why should Mrs. McConkey have had to die? She had never done anyone any harm; she had leant on her counter and chatted with the women and shouted at the wilder kids, sometimes giving one a clout on the ear when he got out of hand, but nothing more. Sadie swallowed, and the sickness passed.

She had a day ahead and did not know what to do with it. She would have liked to be able to go and visit Kevin, to sit by his bedside for half an hour and talk to him. But she could not.

She suddenly thought of Mr. Blake. She would go and talk to him.

Chapter Thirteen

The dog, who was sitting on the garden path, saw her first and got up with a welcoming bark. Mr. Blake looked up from his weeding.

"Sadie! Anything wrong?"

"No."

He came to the gate. "You don't look your usual bouncy self."

"It's just that I've got the sack and Mrs. McConkey is dead. Mrs. McConkey kept the shop near us."

"I see."

"I wanted someone to talk to. So I thought I'd come and see you."

"Come in."

They sat in the kitchen. Sadie rested her folded arms on the kitchen table.

"We always used to make fun of Mrs. McConkey," she sighed. "We would shout names at her when we were small and then run like blazes before she could get hold of us. She never did because she was too fat. And now she's dead."

"Aye, it's bad, Sadie, there's no denying it. Scarcely a day goes by without somebody getting killed, but when it's a person you know it's not so easy to take."

"It's not easy at all," said Sadie. She told him then about the woman in the hat department. "I don't know what I'm going to do now. I'll have to get something else before I tell my mother."

Mr. Blake looked thoughtful. He stroked the dog's coat, flattening the fur until Jack purred contentedly.

"Sadie, I could be doing with a bit of help. I used to have a daily woman and then she got a bad back and couldn't come any more. I could only afford to pay you for mornings but it would be better than nothing, wouldn't it?"

"Mr. Blake, do you mean you'd like me to work for you?"

Mr. Blake laughed at Sadie's astonished face. "Why not?"

"But I'm not very good at that sort of thing. I got the lowest marks in my class for Domestic."

"Marks don't always mean anything. I wouldn't want all that much done. A bit of clearing up and washing and maybe you could cook my lunch?"

"Are you serious?"

"Absolutely."

"All right," she said slowly, trying to adjust to the idea of herself being domesticated. "I'll have a go."

"Good! It'll cheer me up to see you coming in every morning. The other woman had a long face and was always complaining about her back."

"You don't need any cheering up, Mr. Blake," said Sadie, making him laugh again.

They agreed on rates of payment; and in addition Sadie was to be given her lunch and bus fares.

She said she would like to start work straight away. Her earlier mood was forgotten; she was gripped now by a fever for action. Mr. Blake went back to his gardening, leaving her to examine the array of vacuum cleaners, mops and dusters. She decided to scrub the kitchen floor first, not that it looked as if it really needed it, but because it was the kind of job that made her feel virtuous and hard-working. For Mr. Blake she wanted to be hard-working. She sang as she scrubbed and found pleasure in sitting back on her heels afterwards to look at the gleaming wet floor. Her mother would never believe it! The thought of her mother spurred her on. She vacuumed and dusted the sitting room, lifting all the photographs and replacing them carefully. It was funny how she did not mind doing these jobs in someone else's house. She would have hated it at home. And when she looked out of the window she saw Mr. Blake bending and stooping and pottering about. It was very much better than the hat department.

For lunch she cooked mince and potatoes and carrots. The mince was slightly burnt and the carrots a little hard but Mr. Blake declared that he did not mind a bit, in fact he rather liked well-done mince.

"I'll get better with practice," promised Sadie.

After lunch they took Jack for a walk. There was a park close by in which the dog could run freely off the leash. He knew most of the small children playing under the eye of their mothers. He trotted round sniffing and licking them.

"There's Moira Henderson," said Mr. Blake, when they came to the swing park. He nodded at a pretty dark-haired girl in her twenties who was sitting on a bench with a baby on her knee. She was watching two smaller children on the swings. "She's a neighbour of mine. Nice girl. Come on and meet her."

He introduced Sadie and Moira and then they all sat together on the bench. The baby was pressing up on to his feet, treading his mother's lap, pulling at her hair with his small fat fist. From time to time she called out to the other two children. "Watch what you're doing, Peter. No higher, Deirdre!"

"Not much peace, have you, Moira?" said Mr. Blake.

"No," she said with a laugh.

They walked back home with her and the children. Deirdre put her hand into Sadie's and clung to it tightly. She looked up from time to time into Sadie's face. "You seem to have made a new friend," said Mr. Blake. When they reached the Hendersons' gate Moira asked them to come in for a cup of coffee.

Her sitting room was identical in size and shape to Mr.

Blake's, but very differently furnished. It was modern and colourful, and instead of photographs, paintings covered the walls.

"What lovely paintings!" cried Sadie. They looked vivid and exciting to her: they were alive.

"Moira did them," said Mr. Blake. "She's a painter."

"Was, you mean!" said Moira. "I don't get time any more."

"You will again, one of these days."

"In five years time! By then I'll probably have forgotten how to hold a brush."

Sadie and Mr. Blake stayed for an hour. "That was good crack," said Sadie on the way back to his house. "I like a good chat and I liked Moira."

"I thought you would."

"I saw she'd a crucifix in the hall. Is she a Catholic then? She didn't look all that like one."

Mr. Blake was amused. "Yes, she's a Catholic."

"I thought the place would have been smothered with holy pictures and statues."

"You've got some funny ideas, Sadie. By the way, Mike, Moira's husband, is a Protestant."

"Is that right? She seems happy."

"I think she is. Oh, I don't suppose everything's a bed of roses all the same—that would be too much to expect—but they survive all their troubles."

They went up Mr. Blake's path, into the house. "It's easier if you're middle-class," said Sadie. He looked at her. "A Protestant and Catholic getting married, I mean," she added.

Mr. Blake nodded. "Yes, I know. It's fair comment. Some of the people round here might not be too fond of a mixed marriage but it's not likely they're going to chuck a petrol bomb through their window."

"That's what'd happen if you were to do it in my street."

Sadie thought about Moira and Mr. Blake all the way home on the bus. It had been a most interesting day. She was in high spirits when she swung open the kitchen door.

Her mother and father sat at the table looking grim-faced.

"What's up?" asked Sadie.

"That might be for you to tell us," said her father.

"It would be nice not to have to depend on Linda Mullet for all our information," said her mother.

Sadie sat down. "Linda Mullet? What's she been saying now?"

"She told us you'd got the sack," said Mr. Jackson.

"Is that all?"

"What do you mean—is that all?" demanded Mrs. Jackson. She pursed her mouth. "What else could she have told us?"

"Nothing. Anyway, I've got another job." Sadie told them about Mr. Blake and his villa, how she had washed the floor and cooked the dinner.

"You're joking," said her mother. "You doing domestic work? I don't believe it."

"Well, you'll have to," said Sadie, "for it's true."

Next morning she cleaned Mr. Blake's windows, inside and out. She rubbed till her elbow was tired and the glass glistened. Then she stepped back to admire the shine, reaching out here and there to obliterate any traces of a smear.

"Does it give you a glow of satisfaction?"

Sadie looked round to see Moira Henderson at the gate, with her three children.

"Yes," she said, "it does."

"Good." Moira laughed.

Sadie went down the path, polish in one hand, rag in the other, and leant on the gate to talk to Moira.

"I wish I could get a glow of satisfaction out of housework," said Moira. "Maybe I don't do it well enough."

"I expect you get that from your painting?"

Moira nodded. "That's why I miss it so much."

"I was thinking about it on the way home on the bus last night," said Sadie. "And I thought I could look after your kids in the afternoons until I get another job and you could paint."

"Sadie, what a great idea! I'd pay you of course."

"Oh no."

"Oh yes! I've been vaguely thinking of getting someone to look after the kids. Mike's always going on to me about it and I never do anything. He's keen for me to start painting again."

They shook hands on the bargain over the top of the gate. Sadie began at the Hendersons after lunch the same day. At tea-time she anounced that she now had two jobs.

"I'm working as a nanny in the afternoons," she said loftily.

"Minding kids?" said her mother. "You?"

"Why not? I've been a kid myself, haven't I?"

"And never out of mischief," groaned her mother. "If there was any trouble going in the neighbourhood I could be sure you were there."

"Best experience there is for looking after kids," said Sadie. "I know what they're going to do before they do it."

"I should think Sadie would keep them in line all right," said Tommy.

Mrs. Jackson scratched the scalp between her rollers. "Honest, Sadie Jackson, I never know what you're at from one day to the next."

Just as well, thought Sadie, thinking of Kevin, and unconsciously smiling. Her mother, noticing her smile, frowned suspiciously.

On Friday, Kevin came to Mr. Blake's. He still had the bandage round his head and a slight limp but apart from that was almost back to normal.

"You look a new man," said Sadie, taking his hands in hers.

"I've been resting." He grinned. "Every time I moved two yards my mother yelled at me. What have you been doing?"

"Not resting. Wait till you hear!"

Mr. Blake took Jack out for a long walk before supper. Sadie and Kevin sat on the settee and she gave him an account of her week.

"Sounds like you know half the neighbourhood by now."

"I like to pass the time of day when I go in and out of the shops."

"In other words, you're a blether!"

They laughed together. She rested her head against his shoulder. She felt happy.

"Maybe it's as well I nearly collapsed along by the Lagan," said Kevin. "Though at the time I didn't think so!"

"Mr. Blake is the best thing that ever happened to us."

"We must be careful that no one gets to know about him and us."

Sadie nodded. "You're right there."

Chapter Fourteen

Kevin was not allowed to go back to work for another two weeks. His job involved too much heavy lifting, the doctor said. The days were long for Kevin. The house was too small; the street, in the daytime hours, was the prerogative of the women and young children. The women gossiped in their doorways, arms folded, their eyes sharp for any speck of interest. When he came by they called out to him, willing him to stop, but he seldom did. He talked less to anyone now than he ever had.

"There's a real change come over your Kevin," said Mrs. Kelly to Mrs. McCoy when she called to see her. "He used to be a right cheery boy, always ready for a bit of a crack."

Mrs. McCoy lifted another shirt from the wash basket and carried on ironing. She was hot, even though the back door stood wide open to let in the air, or what air there was in the small spaces between the houses. She thought of the green fields of County Tyrone and thought she must try to take the baby there for a week or two after he was born so that his lungs could fill with fresh country air.

"Kevin got a right beating up, you know."

"There's some that say he was asking for it."

Mrs. McCoy lifted her head and looked Mrs. Kelly straight in the eye. "And what are you meaning by that?"

Mrs. Kelly shrugged, looked away. "Well ... you know."

"Because he went out a couple of times with a Protestant girl? It might have been silly of him but it's not a crime," said Mrs. McCoy. "Not even our church says it's a crime."

"Oh, I wasn't saying it's a crime," said Mrs. Kelly hastily. "It's just that with all the trouble round here and all that ..."

Mrs. McCoy folded the shirt neatly, laid it aside, reached for another. She straightened her back, putting her hand to her hip.

"Are you all right?" asked Mrs. Kelly.

"Yes. Just a bit tired."

"Come on, let me do some of that for you."

Mrs. McCoy protested, she did not like to sit idle anyway, but Mrs. Kelly insisted. She was a good-hearted woman, thought Mrs. McCoy, as she sat back in the armchair to take a rest. She would always come if you needed her. She had only three children and Kate was the youngest so she had more time to ·spare than most of the other women.

Mrs. Kelly slapped the iron up and down the ironing board. The clothes might not be as smoothly pressed this time but no matter. Mrs. McCoy suddenly realised how tired she was. And she had a pain in her back.

"He's not going out with her now then, I take it?" asked Mrs. Kelly.

"Not as far as I know. But I don't ask him where he's going every time he goes out. He's too old for that."

"Oh, of course. But I was just wondering. He doesn't see much of Kate now. They used to be that close at one time."

"I wouldn't think of asking him about Kate, Mrs. Kelly. And I'm sure you'd agree that you and I shouldn't talk about them either." Mrs. McCoy stood up and rubbed her back. "Do you know, I think I'm going to have to ask you to phone for the ambulance and take me to the hospital?"

The other woman dropped the iron.

"Don't get flustered now," said Mrs. McCoy. "This is my ninth after all so I know what I'm doing but I'd just like to have it in the hospital. I have my bed booked after all." To have the baby at home would mean missing those few lovely days of peace and rest with the order of the hospital around her and the friendly attention of the bustling, cheerful nurses.

"Where the devil's Kevin?" said Mrs. Kelly.

"He went out early on. He might not be back for hours."

"Sure he could have run to the phone while I stayed with you."

"But he isn't here," said his mother. "After all, he wasn't to know I'd be needing him."

Kevin was walking in the park with Sadie and Moira's two older children. He had taken to coming over to the neighbour-hood most days. He would arrive about mid-morning at Mr. Blake's in time to have a cup of coffee with them and then he would wash Mr. Blake's car or potter round the garden. He was so unused to gardens that the very feel of soil and grass felt strange to his fingers. When he lay on the ground up on Cave Hill he did not actually put his fingers into the earth.

In the afternoons he went with Sadie to collect the children. He felt safe with Sadie in the district: they could walk without looking over their shoulders. No one knew them. In his own street he felt that eyes followed him as he walked. At every corner he braced himself, half expecting to be jumped on. When he came to meet Sadie in the evenings he left his own neigh-bourhood by devious routes, feeling partly annoyed that he should have to be bothered by such tricks, partly enjoying the exercise of outwitting possible shadowers. There was a bit of him that enjoyed excitement, even danger. Sadie understood it, shared it. It added spice to their meetings, made them laugh together.

When he was coming home at tea-time that day he met Kate. She hailed him as he was coming off the bus. He stood and waited for her reluctantly.

"Your mother's had her baby," said Kate. "A wee girl. They were looking all over for you this afternoon and they couldn't find you anywhere. They had to get Brede from the nursery to look after the wee ones."

"I must be getting home then."

"Hey, wait for us," said Kate. "It's a bit late to be running now. What do you do with yourself all day?"

"Nothing much."

"You must do something."

He shrugged. He slowed his step to let Kate walk beside him. She would run if he did not. She could hang on like a dog with its teeth on a bone.

"You don't seem to have much time for your old friends now."

"Some of them are no longer my friends." Kevin touched his bandage. "I don't like getting kicked in the head."

"It wouldn't be friends that did that."

"Kate, I know who did it."

"You're thinking of Brian Rafferty, aren't you? He says you've been going round slandering him. He's not pleased."

"I don't care if he's pleased. You keep out of it, Kate."

They reached the scrapyard. She put her hand on his arm. "Just a minute, Kevin. I want a word with you."

"All right." He sighed inside himself.

"Is it all over with us?" Her blue eyes were round and tearful, framed by the false eyelashes that he had often called road sweepers.

"But Kate..." He bit his lip. "Well, it's not as if we were going steady or anything."

"I thought we were going steady," she cried.

"But I didn't," he said bluntly.

"You're cruel and horrible, Kevin McCoy, and I hate you!"

"Now look, Kate—"

She was gone, running towards her house, crying no doubt, ready to fall into the arms of her mother. It was as well that she had gone for he had not known what else to say to her. What could he say? He hated it when girls cried. He was uncomfortable, did not know what to do. He had never seen Sadie cry. Brede wept sometimes, very quietly, deep down in her bed.

He continued up the road to his house. Brede was there cooking the meal, keeping the children in order. She had been given a week's leave from the nursery to look after the family.

"Where have you been?" she asked, pushing a lock of hair back from her hot forehead with the back of her hand.

"Don't you start!" he answered irritably.

"Why, who else has been at you?"

"I met Kate Kelly on the way up."

Brede sighed. "Have you been upsetting her?"

"Can I help it?" he demanded.

"No. But it might not do you any good."

"If you're suggesting I keep in with her because of my job you should know better than that! Kelly employs me because I work hard, not because his daughter's after me." He sat down at the table and straightened his leg. It still ached if he walked too much.

Brede hesitated. "She can cause trouble, Kate, if she wants to."

"Let her. I'll not be blackmailed."

"I've seen her around with Brian Rafferty quite a bit."

"Maybe they'd suit one another."

"You sound sour tonight."

"I'd just like to be left alone for a while."

Brede turned down the gas under the pot on the stove and began setting the table. "Were you out seeing Sadie?" Kevin did not answer. "Be careful, Kevin, won't you? It's all right, you know you can trust me."

"Yes, I know that. You're about the only one I can. Apart from Sadie." And Mr. Blake and Moira Henderson. They were to be trusted too.

Brede raised her eyes to his. "So you are seeing her? Well, I suppose I knew it. You're keen on her, Kevin, aren't you?"

"Would I see her if I weren't?"

Their father came in. He was in a jovial mood. He had been

in the pub 'wetting the baby's head'. It was a tradition to celebrate the birth of a new child by buying your friends a few drinks. By tomorrow he would be grumbling about having another mouth to feed but this evening he was feeling happy and patting his children on the head and telling them what a fine bunch of kids they were.

After tea he went off to the hospital with Brede to see his new child. Kevin stayed at home with the rest of the family. He had not arranged to meet Sadie that evening. Her aunt and uncle were coming on a visit and she said her mother was getting so annoyed with her that she thought she had better stay at home for once.

"Dead boring it'll be," Sadie had said, and Kevin grinned at the picture of Sadie sitting in the front parlour trying to make polite conversation with her aunt.

"So you're working for a man, Sadie?" said her Aunt May. "Well, well!"

"He's old," said Mrs. Jackson sharply. "And he used to teach Sadie at the school. Have another sandwich, May."

"Don't mind if I do. Though I should be watching my figure. Bert says I'm getting as fat as a pig."

Her husband had gone to the pub with Mr. Jackson. Sadie sat with her mother and aunt shifting around on the scratchy plush armchair. She hated the furniture in the front room.

"Can you not sit still for a minute, Sadie?" said her mother.

"She never could sit still, could she, Aggie, from the minute she was born?" Aunt May bit deep into a sandwich. "Are you liking your job then, Sadie?"

"It's great."

"It's only temporary, of course, May," said Mrs. Jackson. "She's just doing it while she looks out for something better."

"But I like what I'm doing," said Sadie, sitting up straight.

"But you could be making bigger wages doing something else. You don't think you can go on bringing that amount of money in every week, do you? I don't think you've any idea what it costs to feed you, my girl." Mrs. Jackson folded her arms. "Oh no, you can't keep on with those two bits of jobs. And there's no use starting to tell me you'll leave home or any of that nonsense for you know fine well you couldn't live in digs on that kind of money."

Sadie got up. "I'm going out," she said.

She shut the sitting door behind her and stood in the narrow hall with rage searing inside her. There was a time when she would have been tempted to kick the door and shout. Now she took a few deep breaths and said some words inside herself.

"You have your hands full there, Aggie," she heard Aunt May saying.

"The job thing is only the least of it," said her mother. "Wait till you hear the rest!"

Sadie did not wait; she left the house. She walked up the street. Mrs. Mullet was at her door, in usual posture, arms folded, one hip leaning against the door jambs, her feet enveloped in fur slippers. Sadie did not look over at her.

She went along the main road to the café where she had taken Brede. She had seen little of her friends in the last few weeks. The café was quiet. Two boys sat in one corner; Linda sat with Steve in another. Sadie went to the counter for a cup of coffee.

"Haven't seen you for ages," said the man as he set the cup on the counter. "Thought you'd deserted me."

"I've been busy."

Sadie carried her coffee to a table. Linda and Steve got up and came across to her.

"Mind if we join you?" asked Linda.

Sadie shrugged.

They sat down.

"Not out with your Mick boyfriend the night?" said Linda, taking a strand of hair and twirling it round one finger.

Sadie eyed her warily. She was glad that Tommy had at last

seen the light and given her up but she knew that Linda blamed her for it, and not Tommy.

"You needn't pretend you don't know who we're talking about," said Linda.

"I've nothing to talk to you about, Linda Mullet." Sadie pushed back her chair.

"Not so fast," said Steve, putting out his arm to block her path. "There's some of us round here don't like the company you keep."

"You can lump it then," snapped Sadie.

"I don't think that's a very nice attitude to take," said Steve, with an unpleasant smile.

"And I don't like anyone telling me what to do. Excuse me."

Steve did not move his arm. He continued to stare at her, daring her to push him. The proprietor lifted the lid of his counter and crossed to their table.

"What's going on here?" He looked at Steve. "Don't you try to be rough with anyone in my café, boy!" He was a big, powerfully-built man; at one time he had been an amateur all-in-wrestler.

Steve shrugged one shoulder but withdrew his hand. He stood up, knocking over his chair. "Come on, Linda, let's blow. This joint's just a dump."

"Come back and pick up the chair." The man's voice was quiet.

Steve ambled on towards the door. Linda stood hesitantly, terrified either to go or to stay.

"Come back!" The proprietor caught Steve by the shoulder. Steve stopped, facing out to the street. "Now pick up that chair. You knocked it over. I like some manners round here."

Steve picked up the chair. His face was scarlet. As he turned to leave the café he gave Sadie a backward, murderous look. Linda followed him.

"Lout!" said the proprietor. "You all right, Sadie?"

"Fine, fine," she assured him. She could easily have got

away from Steve herself. Now he had something else chalked up against her.

The proprietor accompanied her out on to the pavement to make sure that Steve and Linda were not about.

The evening stretched emptily ahead. She wished she had arranged to meet Kevin. She wondered what he would be doing. The thought of the house with Aunt May twittering away made her shudder. She wandered around the streets. She always walked when she was restless. She came eventually to the edge of their quarter and stood looking at the barbed-wire barricades. Beyond them was Kevin. She longed to see him. But he was unreachable.

"I'm glad Ma's well," said Kevin.

"Oh, she's doing rightly," said his father.

"And so is the baby," said Brede with a smile. "Just a wee wisp of a thing. You forget how little they are when they're newly born."

They sat round the kitchen table drinking tea and eating soda bread that Brede had baked earlier. The younger children were all in bed and the house was quiet.

Mr. McCoy yawned and stretched. "I'm thinking we could be doing with an early night. After all the excitement."

The front door opened and they heard Uncle Albert's voice. "Are you in?"

"Come in, Albert," shouted back Mr. McCoy.

Uncle Albert poked his head round the kitchen door. "The army's having a search," he announced.

They all got up at once.

"In this street?" asked Mr. McCoy.

"The very one," said Uncle Albert.

They went to the front door. Most of their neighbours were gathered at their doors already.

"I'm blowed if they're going to poke inside my house," said Mr. McCoy. He pulled his door shut behind him and stood feet astride on the pavement.

"You can hardly stop them," said Brede quietly. "And we've nothing to hide."

They saw two armoured cars and several figures in khaki at the end of the street.

"I heard tell they'd had a tip off," said Uncle Albert. He shook his head. "There's informers everywhere."

"So they must be expecting to find something," said Brede.

"They'll not find anything," said Mr. McCoy. "They just take it into their heads to have a search if they've nothing else to do of an evening."

Kevin said nothing. He left them and sauntered slowly down the street. The first three houses had been searched. The soldiers had come out empty-handed. Some women were shouting at them, a few teenage girls ran alongside calling out obscene names. The soldiers strode on as if they were deaf.

Another house: another blank. There was one more house before they would reach Raffertys'. Kevin scanned the crowds in the street. No sign of Brian or his father, though Mrs. Rafferty stood at her door, fire in her eyes, ready to lash out with her tongue at the searchers when they arrived.

The soldiers came out of the adjoining house. Kevin saw Brian then; he was turning the corner to come in to the street. Kevin looked back over at the Raffertys' house. Their turn had come.

Chapter Fifteen

Mrs. Rafferty, after her initial tirade, stood to one side and allowed the soldiers to enter.

"If you want to waste your time that's up to you," she shouted after them. "Eejits!"

Brian came and stood beside Kevin, with his thumbs tucked into his belt. His jaw moved slackly from side to side, over a wad of chewing gum. He made no move to cross the street to join his mother. Kevin glanced sideways at him.

"Aren't you worried?"

"What have I to be worried about?"

"You should know."

Brian laughed softly.

The searchers were spending longer in the Raffertys' house than in any other that they had been in. It looked to Kevin as if they had been tipped off.

"Can't trust anyone these days," said Brian, shaking his head. "Boys, what a life! An informer would look you in the eye as easy as stab you in the back."

"I hope you're not looking at me," said Kevin quietly. "I hate your guts but I wouldn't inform on you."

"Expect me to believe that?" Brian spat his chewing gum into the gutter.

"Believe whatever you like, I'm not interested in what cowards believe."

"Cowards?" Brian swung round, eyes blazing.

"Yes, cowards. Anyone who has to bring two helpers to beat up one person is yellow right to the middle."

At that moment the soldiers clattered out of the Raffertys' house. They were empty-handed.

"Satisfied?" demanded Mrs. Rafferty.

They did not answer; they went on to the next door. Brian Rafferty laughed, a loud triumphant laugh that made his mother look at him.

"Where have you been?" she called. "And where's your da? That's what I'd like to know. He'd have given those louts hell if he'd been here. Come on in for your supper."

"Go on to your mammy," said Kevin.

Brian glowered.

"Come on this minute," said his mother, and he went.

Kevin limped back up the street. The soldiers went from house to house, followed by a crowd of jeering children. They came eventually to the McCoys'.

Mr. McCoy blustered for a few minutes, with Uncle Albert putting in some remarks, and then Brede put her hand on her father's arm. "Might just as well let them," she said. "Save a lot of time."

The soldiers were quiet and solemn. Theirs was a difficult job. They had to keep their tempers whilst all around were losing theirs.

They searched the McCoys' house and found nothing. Kevin sighed with relief, not that he had any reason to feel guilty, but for a few minutes, when they were inside, it had come to him that Brian Rafferty might have planted his gun in their backyard or under the stairs. It would be easy enough to do: their door was unlocked all day.

The whole street was searched and not a thing found. The soldiers drove off to a chorus of booing and abuse, and a hail of stones.

"They've only got what they asked for," declared Mr. McCoy.

The neighbours were angry. Voices were raised in the street for a full hour afterwards.

"Certainly it's not a nice thing to have your home pulled over," said Brede with a sigh, as they sat in the kitchen drinking another cup of tea.

"I thought an Englishman's home was meant to be his castle," said Uncle Albert.

"That's if you're an Englishman," said Mr. McCoy. "If you're an Irishman it's a different matter. You get treated like dirt by everyone."

"I'm away to bed," said Kevin.

He lay in bed listening to the voices outside. Most he knew well for he had been listening to them for nearly eighteen years. He was just on the borders of sleep when the armoured cars returned to the street. The noise made him blink, and sleep slipped away. What was up now?

The cars were stopping outside their house. Feet clattered on the pavement, voices rang out. Kevin sat up, resting on one elbow, frowning. Gerald sat up too and nipped out of bed to go to the window.

"There's soldiers at our door," said Gerald. He hung out of the window with an imaginary machine gun in his hands and sprayed them below, making the sound of machine gun fire.

"Quit it, Gerald," said Kevin.

He pushed back the bedclothes and joined Gerald at the window. The door had been opened now and the men were holding a conversation with Mr. McCoy.

"Don't be so daft," Mr. McCoy was saying. "Away and have your heads examined."

The bedroom door opened behind Gerald and Kevin. Brede slipped into the room.

"The soldiers have come for you, Kevin," she whispered.

"For me? But what—?"

Uncle Albert appeared behind Brede, pushing her aside. "Come on, boy, I'll get you over the back wall while your da keeps them talking."

"What are you talking about?"

"They're after you."

"I haven't done anything." Kevin held out his hands. "You don't think I'm going to go jumping over the back wall in my pyjamas at this time of night, do you?"

"Better that than end up in the jail," said Uncle Albert.

But the soldiers were in the house by now anyway. Kevin started to dress. "Don't worry," he said to Brede. "There's some mistake. I haven't been in any trouble."

"Kevin." Mr. McCoy came panting up the stairs.

"I'm coming."

"Now then, don't get excited, son. We'll get you out of this somehow."

"It's not me that's excited. And when I find out what I'm supposed to be in then we can talk of getting out of it."

Kevin went down to the front room. Three soldiers stood there looking large in the small space. A box was lying on the table: it was the box that had been under Brian Rafferty's bed. Kevin half closed his eyes.

"You recognise it, I see?" said the officer.

"You see nothing of the kind," said Mr. McCoy.

"I'd prefer to speak to your son, Mr. McCoy." The officer looked at Kevin. "Do you know what's in this box?"

Kevin swallowed. "No."

The officer flipped it open so that they could see the gun and ammunition.

"You didn't find that in this house," said Mr. McCoy. "And you're not going to get away with pretending that you did."

"I haven't said that." The officer was keeping his eyes on Kevin's face. "We found it in Kelly's scrapyard."

"And what's that to do with us?" demanded Mr. McCoy.

"Your son works there."

"He hasn't been at work this past two weeks. He got beat up by a gang of thugs. Look at him!"

"But you've got a key to the yard, haven't you?" the officer asked Kevin.

"Yes."

"So what does that prove?" said Mr. McCoy.

"Nothing," said Uncle Albert. "Not a blinking thing. Sure ould Kelly must have half a dozen keys to his yard."

"Half the time the place isn't locked up anyway," said Mr. McCoy. "Anyone could shin over the wall even if it was."

Kevin said nothing. He felt as if his lips were frozen, as if he were caught up in a nightmare in which he found that he was unable to speak. Found guilty by his silence.

"We have reason to believe that your son hid this box in the scrapyard, Mr. McCoy," said the officer.

"Reason? You'd believe anything it'd suit you to believe."

"What have you to say?" the officer asked Kevin.

Kevin moistened his lips. "I know nothing about it."

"You were seen taking the box into the yard."

"Seen?" Kevin found his voice coming back with a surge of anger. "By whom?"

"We will discuss that at the police station. I think it would be better. But we do have a witness."

"A witness?" said Brede. The quietness of her voice made the soldier pause.

"I think we have a right to know who it is," said Mr. McCoy.

"It might be better not. We don't want reprisals or anything like that."

"It wouldn't be Kate Kelly, would it?" asked Brede.

The officer started.

"So it was," said Brede.

"How did you know?"

"Instinct."

"She's got a fine instinct," declared Mr. McCoy. "Just like her mother. So that wee brat Kate Kelly's been telling tales, has she?"

"We have to decide if they're lies or not. She was reluctant to reveal your son's name—" He broke off as Kevin laughed derisively. "But she had to protect her father. After all, the box was found in his yard and he could have been blamed for it.'

"So it's her word against mine," said Kevin. "Well, I'll come down to the barracks and you can bring her there and I'll face her with it. You'll see then who's telling the truth."

"I don't know if that'll be possible. She was very upset."

"I bet she was," said Kevin sarcastically.

"You can prove nothing," said Mr. McCoy. "And you can wait on me. I'm coming too."

Brede sat up all night with Uncle Albert waiting for them to come home. The birds began to chirp, the first flushes of colour came into the sky, and still there was no sign of her father and brother.

"They can prove nothing," said Uncle Albert for the hundredth time.

"I think I'll take a walk down and see what's going on," she said when the hands on the red and cream kitchen clock stood at seven.

"I'll come with you, Brede."

"No, no, don't bother, Uncle Albert. You just stay here in case any of the wee ones should wake."

He would be asleep before she returned. As she left the kitchen his eyelids were closing.

She ran all the way to the police station and arrived breathless. She asked the sergeant on duty if she could speak to the officer who had brought in her brother for questioning. At that moment the soldier came out of a room and recognised Brede.

"Can I have a word with you?" asked Brede.

He nodded. He came over to her.

"It's about Kate Kelly. I think you ought to know that she has a grudge against my brother Kevin." Brede gulped and went on, "You see she's rather keen on him and he's given her the go-by. So I don't think you could call her an unbiased witness."

The officer smiled fleetingly. "Perhaps not. As a matter of fact I'd begun to suspect something of the kind. I've been back to talk to her. And your brother's sticking to his statement that he had nothing to do with it."

"I'm sure he had not," said Brede.

"You don't know who did?"

Brede shook her head.

"And if you did you wouldn't say, would you?"

"Well ... I don't know. But since I don't know there's nothing I could tell you anyway. So you'll let my brother go then?"

"We can't keep him. I think he knows something about it but he won't tell us what. No one will ever tell us anything. If you hang on a minute you can go home with him and your father."

"No, I'll not wait. I'd rather you didn't say I'd come and told you about Kate Kelly."

"O.K."

"Thank you."

Brede ran back home. Uncle Albert was snoring, head slumped on the table between his arms. He sat up abruptly when she came in.

"What the devil's going on?"

"It's all right. I think father and Kevin will be coming soon."

They arrived five minutes later. Mr. McCoy had a great deal to say about the police and the British army, slander, injustice, politics, the Border, the English ... Uncle Albert nodded from time to time but was unable to get in a word. Kevin ate the breakfast that Brede cooked for him. He was silent and brooding. He did not even seem to be listening to what his father was saying. Brede was unhappy about the look in his eyes.

He stood up.

119

"Are you going to bed, Kevin?" asked Brede. "It would do you good to have some sleep."

"I don't feel like sleep."

She did not like the sound of his voice either. It was full of foreboding. She said, "But you look dead beat."

"I'm going out." It was an announcement; no one would stop him.

"Well, don't go killing yourself trailing around the streets," said his father, breaking off in the midst of a dissertation on the treatment of Ulster by the Westminster Government. "No wonder a pair of shoes never lasts long on your feet."

Kevin walked out.

"Be careful, Kevin," Brede called after him.

"Albert, they can send the whole of the British army over here and it'll not solve a thing," said Mr. McCoy.

"Aye, you're right, Pete, you're right."

"Da, I'm worried about Kevin," said Brede.

"Sure you're always worrying about something. Just like your mother."

"But I think he's away out to get the one that framed him."

Mr. McCoy turned in his seat. "Kate Kelly."

"Not her."

"Who then? Does he know who put that box in the yard?"

Brede shrugged. Her face flushed. She went to the sink to start the washing up.

"Do you know, Brede?" demanded her father.

"Me? How would I know?" she asked. "I'll just go and take a look for the milkman."

She went out on to the pavement. Kevin was going slowly down the street, sauntering almost, like one who had nothing in particular to do. As he drew level with the Raffertys' house she saw him turn his head and stare at it. She went back inside.

Kevin reached the end of the street, turned the corner into the next one, passed the scrapyard. A few yards along an alley ran between two blocks of houses. He slipped into it and stood with his back resting against the wall. The morning sun was warm on his face. Brian Rafferty should be along in a few minutes on his way to work.

Chapter Sixteen

"You have been warned." Mr. Blake read the last words of the letter and shook his head. "Do you hear that, Jack?" he said. "I have been warned." Jack got to his feet on hearing his name and wagged his tail. "Nobody will tell me what to do, Jack. There's only one thing to be done with anonymous letters. Burn them. We'll burn them all, Jack."

Mr. Blake clicked on his lighter and held the flame to the edge of the paper. The page curled slowly, then burst into fire about half way up. He dropped it on to the grate. The writing on this first letter was different to the one that had come the day before. He took the hearth brush and shovel and swept up the ashes in case Sadie should suspect anything. She was very sharp, and he did not want her to be worried.

He was tipping the ashes into the bucket in the kitchen when the front door bell rang. He looked at his watch. It was a bit early yet for Sadie.

He opened the door and Kevin half fell into the hall. Mr. Blake supported him. There was blood on Kevin's shirt.

"Sorry," said Kevin. "I seem to be making a habit of it. Collapsing on you."

Mr. Blake took him into the sitting room and sat him on the settee.

"I'm all right really," said Kevin. "It looks worse than it is."

"But you've blood on you. Where's it coming from?"

"It's not mine."

"Whose is it then?"

"Fellow by the name of Rafferty, Brian Rafferty. Remember I told you about him?"

"The one with the gun?"

Kevin nodded. He told Mr. Blake what had happened during the night and how in the morning he had waited in the alley for Rafferty and had beaten him up. "It was as if the devil was in me," said Kevin. "You don't think I should have done it, do you?"

"I understand why you did, Kevin."

"But you think it was wrong?"

"I don't like violence of any kind." Mr. Blake lit his pipe. "But it's what you think that counts."

"I don't know what I think." Kevin put his head back against the settee. His face was pale and drawn. "But I feel sick. I felt sick when I stood and looked down at Rafferty. It's not that I care about him very much." He frowned. "I wanted to fight him, I wanted to kill him, but after I'd got him down there lying at my feet I wished I hadn't done it. Do you understand that?"

"Of course."

"It seemed stupid somehow. I don't know. I don't really understand myself. He deserved it after all."

"I suppose you could say he deserved it," Mr. Blake agreed. "But maybe you feel it didn't do you any good beating him up?" The front door bell buzzed. "That'll be Sadie. Shall I tell her about it?"

"Yes," said Kevin, closing his eyes.

Mr. Blake took Sadie to the kitchen to recount the story. He waited patiently between sentences to give her time to explode. If she got hold of Kate Kelly she was going to tear her to ribbons and when she heard that Kevin had beaten up Brian she nodded with satisfaction. "He was needing a lesson," she said.

"It seems that Kevin has got one from it," said Mr. Blake, and went on to tell her of Kevin's reaction.

"But what does he feel like that for?" she demanded. "Rafferty framed him, and don't forget he beat Kevin up before! With two others to help him."

"I hadn't forgotten. Neither had Kevin. But what's the next thing? More blood?"

Sadie bit her lip. "But he couldn't have let Rafferty get away with it."

"It's not Rafferty I'm bothered about. It's Kevin. He's not feeling very happy. Put on the kettle, Sadie, and make him a cup of sweet tea. It might calm the sickness in his stomach."

She made the tea and took a cup to Kevin. He smiled bleakly at her as she sat down beside him.

"I'm a right looking sight," he said.

"You look all right to me. Come on, drink some tea and you'll be feeling better. And then after that you're to lie down in Mr. Blake's bed and take a rest."

"Bossy this morning, aren't you?"

"There's times you need a bit of bossing." She held the cup for him whilst he drank. His own hand shook when he tried to take it from her.

"Maybe I am a bit tired," he said.

Whilst he slept she washed Brian Rafferty's blood out of Kevin's shirt. She watched the dirty water run out down the drain. Water tinged with blood. Suddenly she felt a bit sick herself. She pushed open the windows over the sink. Mr. Blake was in the back garden weeding round his rose bushes. He was proud of his roses; he had told Sadie all the different names though she could not remember them.

"O.K.?" he asked.

She nodded.

She rinsed the shirt three times in clean water, wrung it out and took it to the garden to hang it up to dry. She strung it out, pegged it and stood back to examine it. Not a shadow of a stain.

"I hope he hasn't killed Rafferty," she said to Mr. Blake. "You don't think he would, do you?"

"It's unlikely."

Sadie knelt down beside him. "But he might have. You never know, Rafferty might have hit his head on the ground when he fell."

"It takes a lot to kill a man."

"Not always. It can happen in a second."

"Only with a gun or a knife."

"Kevin didn't have a knife, did he?" said Sadie slowly. "He wouldn't have taken a knife with him, would he?"

"Sadie, you know him better than I do."

"No, he wouldn't have had a knife." She bent over a deep red rose and took a deep breath. "What a smell!"

"It's rich, isn't it?" Mr. Blake smiled. "I must say I enjoy my roses."

"It's nice being in a garden."

"I was thinking it would be a good idea if we were to go out into the country tomorrow. It would do us all good."

"What a lovely idea!" cried Sadie.

Kevin slept through the morning and afternoon. Sadie peeped round the door to look at him before she went to Moira Henderson's, and after she returned. He lay on his back, mouth slightly parted, his long lashes resting on the edge of his cheekbones. She closed the door quietly behind her.

"He's sleeping like a baby," she said to Mr. Blake.

"There's nothing better than sleep for him. Let him lie awhile yet, Sadie."

Her mother was expecting her home to tea but she said that she would come back afterwards. When she got off the bus near her street she saw Tommy coming out of the hardware shop with a bottle under his arm. He waited for her.

"Do you know what this is?" he held up the bottle.

She sniffed. "Smells like turpentine."

"Right first go. Come on and I'll show you why we need it."

"What's the big mystery?"

"Come and see."

He walked past the house, round the corner. He pointed at the gable wall. Below the picture of King Billy someone had written in white paint: A TRAITOR LIVES HERE.

"Honest to goodness!" Sadie rested her hands on her hips.

"Aye, honest to goodness!" said Tommy. "But if we don't get it off here fast two people we know are going to have a stroke." He pulled two rags from his pocket, threw one at Sadie. "Better get started."

"I've a good idea who might have done this," she said, as she scrubbed at the word 'traitor'.

"Done what?" asked her father's voice behind her.

She dropped the rag. "What a fright you gave me!"

"What are you up to?" Mr. Jackson tried to edge round her.

"Some eejit's been writing on our wall," said Sadie. "That's all."

"And what have they been writing?"

"Just a lot of rubbish."

She had obliterated the first three letters of the word. Mr. Jackson stared at the other four.

"We couldn't make out what it was at all," said Tommy, who was scouring the rest of the words.

"Terrible bad writing," said Sadie. "Somebody's dead ignorant obviously."

Mr. Jackson humphed and frowned, then went into the house. Sadie leaned back against the flank of the white horse and let out her breath. "Whew!"

"He knew what the words said, Sadie," said Tommy quietly, "I wish you would give up seeing Kevin before any worse trouble happens."

"I've no intention of stopping seeing him," she said. "Do you think I'd give in that easily?"

Tommy sighed and put some more turpentine on the rag.

Next morning, Sadie got up at the same time as her mother.

"I'm going to work early today," she said. "And I'll be late back tonight."

"What's up today?" Mrs. Jackson cracked an egg and slid it into the frying pan.

"We're going to do some spring-cleaning."

"In July?"

"It doesn't matter when you spring-clean, does it?"

Mrs. Jackson shook her head, cracked another egg. Tommy came into the kitchen yawning. Sadie combed her hair in front of the mirror beside the sink, humming a tune inside her head. It was a lovely morning, it would be fresh and sweet in the country and she would have a whole day with Kevin and Mr. Blake away from the town and all the people she did not want to see. "Don't comb your hair in the kitchen," said her mother, who always combed her hair in front of that mirror and in fact kept it there for that purpose. Mrs. Jackson set a plate of fried potato bread and an egg on the table for Sadie.

Sadie ate quickly and was finished before Tommy's breakfast was ready. She avoided looking at him.

"What are you smiling about?" asked her mother. "I never thought I'd see the day when you'd be grinning about the prospect of spring-cleaning someone's house."

"It's just that it's a nice morning."

She wanted to skip as she went up the street. She did not go round by the side of the house so she did not see that the word TRAITOR had been repainted on the gable wall. She rode out to Mr. Blake's house on the top front seat of the bus pitying all the people she saw hurrying to spend such a day in a dingy shop or office. Her mother thought she was going regularly to the Labour Exchange to look for a new job.

Mr. Blake had taken his car out of the garage before she arrived. It stood in the street looking shiny and clean. Kevin had washed it only two days before.

"Good morning, Sadie." Mr. Blake was cheerful. He always was.

She went straight to the kitchen to start making a picnic

lunch. When Kevin arrived she ran to meet him in the hall.

"How's Rafferty?" she asked at once.

"Still alive."

"Thank goodness for that!"

"But a bit bashed about, so I hear. They tell me he has a few stitches and has taken to his bed."

"Bed'll be a good place for him," said Mr. Blake. "Keep him out of trouble."

His friends would not be lying in their beds though, thought Sadie, but she did not say it for she did not want the day spoiled. Kevin was looking much better. He had slept all night as well, he said.

They loaded up the car and Mr. Blake fetched some maps from his bedroom. They did not know where they were going; they wanted to wander off without any set ideas. Moira Henderson walked along with the baby under her arm to watch them getting ready. Deirdre and Peter played in and out of the car.

"You're lucky to be going away for a whole day," said Moira. "I wouldn't mind it myself."

"Sorry we can't take you all with us," said Mr. Blake. "Not enough room. Unless you'd like to sit on the roof!"

They set off in high spirits. Moira and the children waved until they turned the corner. Kevin and Sadie settled on the back seat to enjoy the trip. Jack lay on the front passenger seat beside his master.

"I think we'll head north," said Mr. Blake. "Up towards the glens of Antrim maybe?"

"Anywhere at all," said Sadie. "I don't mind a bit." Her hand lay in Kevin's. He looked at her and smiled.

They took the road that ran close round by the coast, winding and twisting beside the sea. The water looked green today, tipped with white.

Mr. Blake exclaimed suddenly.

"What's the matter?" asked Kevin, leaning forward.

"Don't know. Just felt a wobble. There it goes again. Think it might be a flat tyre. I'll pull in."

Mr. Blake pulled on the steering wheel, braking gently, and then the car lurched violently, sending them spinning straight across the road. The tyre was not flat: the off-side front wheel careered on down the road leaving the car behind.

Chapter Seventeen

The car lay crushed against the sea wall on its off-side, the near-side wheels spinning in the air. Two cars stopped and the drivers ran to help release the occupants. The dog would not stop barking and yelping. He was trembling with fright. Sadie scrambled out first, and then Kevin. They helped to ease out Mr. Blake. He was dazed and could not stand. They set him down by the edge of the road. Jack sat beside him licking his face.

By now several other cars had stopped, and soon a police car came along the road. The policeman sent out a call for an ambulance.

"I'm all right," Mr. Blake kept muttering.

"We must have you all checked up," said the constable.

Sadie and Kevin were bruised and a little shocked but nothing more. Mr. Blake had kept his head and controlled the car as far as it was possible so that they had not been travelling very fast when they hit the wall.

"Lucky escape," said the constable. "You don't often have much of a chance when a wheel comes off."

"Can't understand it," said Mr. Blake. "A wheel coming off."

"Somebody hasn't tightened it up properly," said the constable. "We'll have to check at your garage."

"Haven't had that wheel changed for months," said Mr. Blake.

"Never mind," said Sadie. "Don't think about it any more just now."

They were taken to the nearest hospital by ambulance. The doctor cleared them but stressed that Mr. Blake should rest for a few days. "After all, you're not twenty any longer," he said. "You're a bit shaken up. But sound as a bell otherwise."

They returned to Belfast by taxi and Sadie insisted that Mr. Blake go straight to bed. He went meekly, falling asleep almost at once.

The police came next morning. There were two of them in plain clothes. Sadie and Kevin looked at one another after the men had shown their cards. Mr. Blake got up and sat in his armchair in the sitting room to receive them.

"I suppose it's about the accident," said Mr. Blake.

"It was no accident," said one, who did most of the talking. The other took notes and watched the faces of Mr. Blake, Kevin and Sadie.

"No accident?" said Kevin.

"No. When the car was examined it was discovered that the nuts of *all* the wheels had been loosened. It was only a matter of time before one or more of the wheels came off."

Sadie held her hands clenched tightly together in her lap. She was thinking of Steve. Could he do a thing like that? Could he really have wanted to kill her, or did he think that only Mr. Blake would be in the car? Was Steve capable of being a murderer? She did not know. She had known him a long time, they had played together, but she did not know what he was capable of.

Beside her on the settee sat Kevin, his forehead creased. He was thinking of Brian Rafferty. Could Brian have come in the night with a spanner and systematically loosened every nut, thinking as he worked in the dark garage of the possible death that would result? No, Brian could not have done it, since he had been in bed, but he might have sent his friends, the two who had beaten Kevin up. Kevin was not sure who they were. He had not seen their faces and they had not spoken. They might be any two boys he had played with or gone to school with or they might never have seen him before. They were anonymous; he could not decide if they were capable of it.

Mr. Blake reached for his pipe, lit it, puffed slowly, staring into the grate. He was thinking of the letters that had come four mornings in a row. 'You have been warned.' He could almost smell the singeing paper. Many wrote letters and did not act, but then some did.

The detective looked from one face to the other.

"Have any of you any idea who might have done this?" he asked.

Sadie started, roused from her thoughts. "No," she said quickly. "I mean, who would want to do a thing like that deliberately?"

"That's what I'm trying to find out. Have you any suggestions, Mr. Blake?"

Mr. Blake shook his head. "I don't know anyone who would want to kill me," he said with a little smile.

"No enemies?"

"Not that I know of."

"Someone must have been after you for something. Are you a member of any political party or organisation?"

"No. I'm not a joining man. Organisations aren't in my line."

"What about you two?" The policeman swung round on Sadie and Kevin. "Do you belong to any groups? Have you ever?"

"I was once a Girl Guide," said Sadie, and Kevin's mouth twitched. "But that's all."

"And you?" The policeman asked Kevin.

Kevin shook his head.

"Perhaps it was just some hooligan and they happened to

pick on me by chance," said Mr. Blake.

"I feel there's more to it than that. You keep your car in the garage at night?" Mr. Blake nodded. The policeman continued, "So some person or persons went to the trouble to get into your garage and loosen all the wheels, doing it carefully, replacing the hub caps, clearing away any evidence afterwards. That's not the work of hooligans. They might break one of your windows or score a knife across the bodywork but they don't plan anything carefully."

"Seems a bit of a mystery then," said Mr. Blake.

"One we intend to clear up if possible. You were lucky you all got out alive. We might have been looking for murderers this morning."

Sadie stirred uneasily. Should she tell him about Steve? But what was there to tell? She had no proof, no idea even if he was guilty.

Kevin thought of Rafferty's gang. Should he give Brian's name to the policemen? But then he would have to say that Brian Rafferty the night before had been lying in his bed too ill to come out. How could he say that there were two other boys who might have been involved but he did not know their faces or their names?

Mr. Blake thought of the letters but there seemed little point in mentioning them. He had burned them anyway so there was no evidence left. And he did not want Sadie and Kevin to be upset by knowing of them.

They all three kept quiet. The detective looked thoughtful.

"I think it would be helpful if I could establish the relationships between the three of you."

"That's easy enough," said Mr. Blake. "Sadie works for me in the mornings, she does a little cleaning and cooking. And Kevin is a friend."

"Of yours or Sadie's?"

"Both."

"I see. Well, let us take down some particulars."

They wrote down Mr. Blake's name, address, age, occupation. Then it was Sadie's turn. She spoke quickly: the police-man wrote slowly and had to ask her to repeat some of the answers.

"Right." The policeman looked at Kevin.

When Kevin gave his address the detective stopped writing. He repeated the name of the street and then Sadie's street.

"I think that's a piece of information you might have given me earlier."

"You didn't ask," said Sadie. "And I didn't think it would be of any interest."

"So you didn't think it would be of any interest? You say you're friends? How many people in your street have friends in his street?"

"Well ... none that I know of."

"Does your family know you're friendly?"

"Sort of."

"Does yours?" he asked Kevin.

"I'm not sure."

"You're not trying to say that either my family or his would try to kill us both to stop us seeing one another?" Sadie burst out.

"I wouldn't have thought so. But families can do strange things when their blood is up."

"Nobody in mine would do such a thing," said Sadie indig-nantly. "I can tell you that for a start."

"And no one in mine," said Kevin.

"What about neighbours?"

He questioned them for another hour, asking who their friends were, insisting on names and addresses. Sadie did not mention Steve and Kevin did not mention Rafferty.

"These are friends," said Sadie. "You're not going to go round questioning them, are you?"

"Probably not. But we'll check records for any trouble-makers. What about enemies?"

Kevin shrugged.

"Never come up against anyone?"

"Oh, well, of course. The odd fight, you know."

"You've got a bandage on your head. Get that in a fight? When? How?"

Kevin told him he had been beaten up by three boys but that he did not know who they were.

"Expect me to believe that?"

"Can't help it if you don't," said Kevin wearily.

At the end of the hour the detective stood up. He said that he would leave it at that mean time, but he would be back.

"I'll go as far as the gate with you," said Mr. Blake.

"Are you sure you can walk that far, Mr. Blake?" said Sadie.

"Yes, yes, now don't fuss, there's a good girl. Go and make us some tea."

Mr. Blake went down the path with the two policemen.

"I presume you have something you want to say to us alone?"

Mr. Blake nodded. He rested against the gate and told them of the letters. "I didn't want Sadie and Kevin to be disturbed by them. They're a nice couple of kids and I want them to have a chance to be friends."

"It would have saved you a lot of trouble if they hadn't, Mr. Blake. And us too. Coming from streets like theirs they must have known it would be like lighting a fuse. Good day, Mr. Blake."

He watched them drive off in their car. Moira was coming along the road with her children. He waited to speak to her.

"I'm glad you and Mike are happy," he said.

She looked at him in surprise.

"Against all the odds," he added.

"We have a few troubles, you know. Sometimes we argue and even fight." She laughed. "But we make it up again. You're looking sad today. Are you still shaken up by your accident?"

"A bit, I suppose. I'm worried for Sadie and Kevin. I don't think they stand much chance. They have too much against them."

"That's why you're helping them, isn't it?"

"Yes, of course. But I like them both too. They've become real friends to me."

He went back to the house. Sadie and Kevin were in the kitchen, their faces serious.

"We've been thinking, Mr. Blake," said Kevin, "and we feel we shouldn't meet one another here any more."

"Why not?"

"We don't want to get you into any more bother," said Sadie. "Sure we all know why the wheels were loosened."

Mr. Blake sighed. "I would be sorry not to see you both. And I'm not afraid to go on having you here. I think it's important to stick to your principles."

"I think we should come less often," said Kevin. "Maybe once in the week, and we'd have to take care not to be seen."

"I'll still come every day and work for you," said Sadie, wondering as she spoke how long she would be able to stall her mother, who again this morning had been asking when she was getting a new job.

"Whatever you think is best," said Mr. Blake. "We could try that for a while and see if things quieten down. Maybe people will lose interest and leave us in peace."

Kevin said that he would telephone Sadie one morning and arrange their next meeting, but riding home on the bus he decided that he would not phone her. He must not see her again. For her sake. He was terrified that something might happen to her. The 'Twelfth' was approaching, and her street would soon be consumed by Orange fever.

He called in at the scrapyard. He would be able to go back to work the following week and was glad of that for time hung like balls of lead round his neck. He saw Mr. Kelly working at the far end of the yard, sorting out parts of an old car.

"Hi there, Mr. Kelly!" Kevin picked his way through the junk towards him.

Mr. Kelly looked up briefly, then returned to his sorting.

"I've come to tell you I'll be fit for work on Monday."

"You needn't bother." Still Mr. Kelly did not look up.

"What?" Kevin frowned. He and Mr. Kelly had always got on well, they had never exchanged a harsh word. "Do you mean you're giving me my cards?"

"Just that." Mr. Kelly wiped his hands on a dirty rag.

"But why?"

"Do you need me to spell it out for you?"

"You don't think I put that box in your yard, do you?"

"Kate said you did. She saw you."

"She's lying!" Kevin spat the words out angrily.

Mr. Kelly looked him straight in the eye for the first time. "So you're calling my daughter a liar, are you?"

"Yes."

"Do you think I would employ a man that calls my daughter a liar?"

"You're not going to employ me again, are you? I can't win either way. O.K., maybe I wouldn't want to work for you if it means keeping on the right side of your daughter."

"There's no call to be rude."

"I'll tell you something though, Mr. Kelly. If you're fond of your daughter I think you should be taking a good look at the company she's keeping. If you don't you might find more boxes of guns hidden in your yard."

Kevin jumped over a back axle and made for the gate. Mr. Kelly called to him to stop but he did not. That would give him something to worry about.

Brede was baking. He smelt it as he came in the door. Her face was flushed as she bent over the oven.

"Well, Brede," he said. "I've just got the sack. What do you think our father's going to say to that?"

"Plenty," said Brede. "But it doesn't surprise me. I was waiting for it to happen."

"I shall go down and have words with Kelly the night," said Mr. McCoy, when he was told the news.

"You'll do nothing of the kind," said Kevin.

"He can't get away with this."

"Of course he can. It's his yard."

"I'll go down and tell him he's a little namby-pamby run by those stupid women he has in his house."

"That's not likely to get Kevin his job back," said Brede.

"I wouldn't want it back now anyway," said Kevin. "Not after what's happened."

"And what are you going to do?" asked his father. "We've another mouth to feed in this family now."

'I'll go down to the Labour Exchange in the morning and see what they've got."

It did not take long to find out. They were sorry but they had nothing at all that they could offer him. He was not apprenticed, he had no trade, three years in the scrap business was not much of a help for anything else, there were not many scrapyards in the city and no one was asking for labour, and unemployment in the province was high, as he must know. Kevin nodded at each piece of information. Before he had gone he had had no hope. He would have to draw the dole and from time to time he might get some casual labouring to do.

He was out of work. The full realisation of it dawned upon him as he walked around the City Hall. Days to fill. He was too restless to lean on street corners with the others. He would walk for miles and end up wearing out shoe leather and that would cost money. Money ... There was seldom enough to go around anyway. And he would have little to spend on himself.

He thought of Sadie and Mr. Blake and wished that he could go out and see them. For a moment he was tempted, but then his resolve hardened and he thought, no, he must not go, he must leave them alone. That way they, at least, might get peace.

Chapter Eighteen

"I wonder why he doesn't phone," said Sadie.

Each morning she dusted the telephone, wondering if it would ring for her that day. But there it sat, black, and squat, and silent.

"He will," said Mr. Blake. "One of these days. Perhaps at the moment it's too difficult. He's got all sorts of things to work out."

"I hope he's all right."

Sadie worried about him but there was nothing she could do. She could not go to his house and ask for him.

"You're quiet these days," said her mother. "Are you sickening for something?"

"No."

"You don't go out much either. It's not like you. Mind you, I'm just as glad you're staying in. It's not safe to be out in the evenings nowadays."

She sat in her bedroom, reading sometimes or writing letters to Kevin that she tore up afterwards, often just sitting staring out through the window at the bunting that linked the houses in the street. The flags were out, and each evening she heard the sounds of bands practising for the big day. Drums beating. Children shouted in the street, excited by the noise and colour.

The army had been reinforced to keep down the amount of trouble.

Kevin might be ill. Or he could have been beaten up again by Rafferty and his gang. Or his house might have been burned down and his family moved away to Tyrone. Or perhaps he just did not want to see her any more. He might have found another girl, one from his own street, whom he could take out without complication. All the possibilities whirled in her mind.

"I'm glad you've stopped seeing Kevin," said Tommy. "You'll forget him after a while. It's just as well."

On the eve of the 'Twelfth' the bonfires were lit. From her window Sadie watched the children lighting the one at the end of the street. The flames leapt high, spitting against the dark sky. The children danced round it singing Orange songs.

The next morning the Jacksons were astir early. Mr. Jackson was walking in the parade. His bowler hat lay brushed and smooth on the hall table. He wore his best navy-blue suit and white shirt, and the sash of his lodge, purple and gold. Mrs. Jackson took out her rollers after breakfast and combed out her hair, then went upstairs to take off her dressing gown and put on her Sunday clothes.

Tommy was going out, just to see the parade pass, but not to take part in it.

"Why don't you go with him?" Mrs. Jackson asked Sadie.

"I've seen it often enough."

"Better for you than sitting in the house brooding. I don't know what's come over you." Mrs. Jackson shook her head.

"When I went out all the time you were always complaining."

But Mrs. Jackson was not listening. She was fussing in front of the mirror, demanding to know if her hair was all right, and her hat.

Mr. Jackson put on his bowler hat and set off up the street to join the other members of his lodge. A little while later Mrs. Jackson and Tommy went out. Tommy avoided Sadie's eye.

Now Sadie was alone. She stood at the front door. The street was empty; nearly everyone was out lining the route to the 'field' at Finaghy. The sky was overcast, threatening rain. 'No Surrender' said the streamer hanging limply across the street. The sound of the bands reached her.

She could not spend the day in this deserted street. She could go to Mr. Blake's but for once did not feel like it. She would be restless in his tidy villa in the suburban road. She would go to Bangor.

The rain started when she got off the bus. She pulled up the hood of her anorak and walked along by the sea wall enjoying the smell of the sea and the fresh whip of the wind in her face.

At the end of the wall she met Kevin. He was leaning against it looking out at the sea.

"Hello," she said.

He turned. "Hello." He smiled.

She leant against the wall beside him.

"Did you know I'd come here today?"

"I had a feeling you might. Come on, let's go and have some coffee and get out of the rain."

He took her arm and led her across the street. The café was full of wet holidaymakers staring miserably at the rain streaming down the windows. Sadie and Kevin sat huddled together in a corner smiling at one another. For a few minutes they said very little, needing time to adjust to seeing one another again. And then Sadie asked him why he had not phoned.

"It seemed wiser," he said.

"But you came today."

"There's days I feel wise and days I don't. But I'm glad to see you again, Sadie."

She was glad too. It rained on and off most of the day but it did not concern them. The hours passed happily and without anxiety.

"I'm out of work, Sadie," Kevin told her. "That's been another of the things that's been bugging me. I don't know what I'm going to do at all. I've even been thinking of going away."

"Leave Belfast you mean?" she cried.

"I might have to."

"I would miss you." The sparkle died in her eyes.

"Don't be sad. This isn't a day for being sad. It'll probably not happen anyway. If I can get work here I'll stay. Let me see you smile." She smiled, and he leaned forward and kissed her.

"I'll smile again if that's what happens," she said.

At the end of the day he took her to the bus station. It would be safer for them to travel home separately, he said. He would take the bus after hers. Sadie agreed with a sigh. It was hard not to be able to ride home on the bus together, hand in hand; it was the right way to finish off such a day.

"Not much is right these days, Sadie," said Kevin.

She touched his face. It had darkened again. She hated to see him like that. She loved his laugh, the mischievous glint in his dark eyes. Some of his gaiety had gone. He was changing.

She put her head against his shoulder and he stroked her hair. His sweater felt rough against her face.

"Being with you feels right, Sadie," he whispered.

"I think so too."

"You must go soon. Your bus is due."

She looked up at him. "When shall I see you? At Mr. Blake's?"

He hesitated for a moment. "All right," he said. "We'll be careful."

"Wednesday?"

"O.K. Off you go!"

He kissed her, then pushed her gently away. He stood in the alley with his back to the wall. The rain had stopped but dark clouds covered the sky keeping the night chill. He stood and thought of Sadie until it was time to go to the bus station and catch the last bus home.

*　　*　　*

142

"Now you'll not forget to be in for the rent and the Insurance?" said Mrs. McCoy.

"Stop fussing, Ma. I've got it all written down." Kevin waved a sheet of paper. "Where to get the butter one pence cheaper, the best day for fish."

"And you can ask Brede about anything I've forgotten."

"You can't have forgotten anything, surely to goodness!"

Mrs. McCoy could never leave her family without checking every detail, taking into account every possible calamity. Mr. McCoy had a week's holiday so they were both going off to Tyrone taking with them the baby and the next two youngest children.

"Are you ready for off then?" asked Uncle Albert, putting his head round the kitchen door.

"Not be a minute, Albert," said Mrs. McCoy, wrapping the baby's feeding bottle in a cloth and putting it into a bulging carrier bag. Then she put out her arms for the baby. Kevin had been holding her.

"There you are." He swung the baby across.

"Careful, Kevin! You nearly stopped my heart there."

"I've held plenty of babies in my time, have I not?"

" 'Deed I suppose you have."

"Mary!" Mr. McCoy was calling from the front street.

"Coming, Pete."

Kevin carried the bag out for her. The other two children were already in the back of the car, climbing over the seat, jumping up and down with excitement.

"It's about time!" said Mr. McCoy, helping his wife to get into the back of the car with the baby. "It'll be dark before we get there."

"It certainly will," said Kevin.

"Oh, I don't know," said Uncle Albert, who had never made the trip to Tyrone without at least one breakdown, but would never in advance admit to it being the remotest possibility. His memory sieved out anything he didn't want to remember. Just as well, thought Kevin, as he watched Uncle Albert cranking up the car. He wished he was like him.

The engine sprang to life. Uncle Albert cocked his head in admiration. "Going as sweet as a bird, eh, Kevin?"

"Sweeter."

Uncle Albert whistled as he put the starting handle back in the boot amongst the collection of luggage. There was nothing dearer to his heart than setting off on a journey. He was always ready to oblige friends or family with a lift.

"You've a full load on there, Uncle Albert," said Kevin.

"Sure she'll take it in her stride."

Kevin waved them off. They would get to Tyrone eventually. Uncle Albert had a way of getting to his destination somehow or other. By the time they did get there his brother would be cursing the car and Albert and his wife and County Tyrone, and Mrs. McCoy and Albert would be paying no attention. Kevin chuckled to himself as he went inside.

It was quiet in the kitchen. The clock ticked on the dresser. The other children were out playing, Brede was at her nursery. He was in charge of the house.

His mother had made a stew and peeled potatoes. He had only to boil the potatoes, she said, and drain them when they were cooked. Tomorrow he would have to peel the potatoes himself and cook the dinner and shop. He had never done any of these things before for Brede had always been the one to help his mother. His father kept himself well away from all women's work. He couldn't boil an egg and was proud of it. "What is the use of keeping women in the house," he said, "if you have to do their work for them?"

Kevin boiled the potatoes but poured off the water too soon so that the potatoes were still hard. He shook his head with disgust when they sat down to eat their dinner.

"I tried them with a knife, like Ma said."

"Never mind." Brede smiled. "We can still eat them. You'll get the hang of it in no time. You've done very well, Kev. I'll wash up afterwards and one of the others can dry. You'll be going out?"

He nodded.

It was Wednesday. He went out every Wednesday. He met Sadie at Mr. Blake's. They arrived and left at different times and sat in the kitchen at the back of the house. He spent Saturdays with Sadie too. They met outside the city somewhere, usually in the country, well away from people. Sadie brought food and drink and many days they saw no one else at all. They waded in streams, climbed trees, lay in meadows in the sun listening to the continuous chorus of the birds. Long summer days at the end of which he returned home flushed with air and contented. He knew that Brede suspected he was meeting Sadie again though they never mentioned it. Sometimes she would put her hand on his arm and say, "Take care," but that was all.

"She's a fine sister to have," he said to Sadie that evening. "I hope she gets a good man. She'll marry in a year or two, I fancy, and have lots of kids."

"Just like your mother."

"I hope it won't be just the same. My mother's had too much work and not enough living."

"Well, there's one thing for sure," said Sadie, "I'm not going to end up like my mother!"

Kevin laughed. "I think you're safe on that one."

"She found me a job. You'll never guess?" Sadie rolled her eyes. "Working at the cash desk at the local butcher's. Can you imagine me sitting cooped up in one of those wee boxes all day taking the money for lumps of meat?"

"What are you going to do about it?"

"I've done it. I went along for an interview and I told the butcher that the sight of blood always made me vomit. He said that under the circumstances it might not be wise for me to take the job. I said that unfortunately I was forced to agree."

Kevin ruffled her hair. "It takes a lot to put you down, doesn't it, Sadie Jackson?"

"That's what my mother says too!"

They were laughing when Mr. Blake came into the kitchen

with Jack. They had been for a walk and were both thirsty. Sadie got up to put on the kettle and Kevin filled the dog's dish with fresh water.

"It's nice to hear the two of you laughing," said Mr. Blake, hanging up the lead on the back of the door. "Whatever happens we mustn't forget how to laugh."

Kevin came out of the supermarket with a heavy bag in either hand. The greengrocer's next door was not doing any business today: the window had been smashed and broken glass lay amongst the boxes of oranges and apples and carrots. The shop had been looted after the window was broken. Split bananas and squashed tomatoes mingled with the shiny splinters on the floor. He walked on, came to the newsagent's and tobacconist's. Another shattered window, already boarded up. There had been rioting for several hours the previous night. He had lain awake listening to it, wondering if any minute they would have to get up and dress and leave their home for some safer place. Rubber bullets lay in the gutter and at the side of the pavement. He kicked one aside with his foot.

He looked out across the street at the barbed-wire barricades, a burnt-out bus turned over on its side, two armoured cars parked close together with half a dozen soldiers nearby, guns held at the ready. Chaos and destruction. He was sick of it. Sick of it.

He continued through the streets towards his own, skirting patches of pavement where the paving stones had been lifted. He stepped back to let a horde of small screaming children pass. They brandished home-made guns and pieces of stick high in the air. Whooping and yelling, on they went. Yelling for blood.

As he reached the scrapyard he looked sideways through the open gate. Mr. Kelly was there sifting through junk. He glanced up at Kevin.

"Hey, Kevin!"

Kevin stopped.

Mr. Kelly came running.

Kevin set down the two bags and flexed his wrists.

"I was wanting a word with you, son." Mr. Kelly cleared his throat. "It's just that I'd like you to come back and work for me."

Kevin stared at him for a moment, then said, "No thanks."

"Now look here, Kevin boy, we all make mistakes in our time. I'm right sorry about that gun business. I don't believe you did it at all. Could you not be forgiving me?"

"I have forgiven you."

"That's all right then. Will you come back? I'm needing you and I miss your company when I'm out with the truck. We always got on fine together, didn't we?"

"Yes."

"What do you say, Kevin?" Mr. Kelly rubbed his hands together with an air of nervousness. "I'll put up your wage."

"I'm sorry. No."

"But why not?"

"I just don't want the job back. The less of these streets I see the better."

Kevin walked on.

Mrs. Rafferty was at her door. "Morning, Kevin," she called out.

"Good morning, Mrs. Rafferty."

"Getting in the messages then? You'll be a right good house-wife in no time at all." She laughed, a high-pitched laugh that followed him the rest of the way along the street.

He shut the door of the house tight behind him. It was not often that they closed the door in daytime but today he wanted to shut out the world.

He unpacked the bag, put away the things in the cupboard. The list lay on the table. Insurance day. The Insurance man would call and he would take the money from the vase on the mantelpiece and the man would make some crack about Kevin in the kitchen. He could stand the cracks, but the restlessness inside him and the disgust he felt for what was happening all around were different matters. It was as if a boil was building up in the middle of him, getting bigger and bigger every day. He knew it was only a matter of time before it would burst.

Chapter Nineteen

There were disturbances in the night: the sound of gunfire, rumble of armoured cars, shouting in the distance, the flicker of flames against the sky. No one in the Jackson house slept very much. Their own street was quiet but the activity on the fringe of the area kept them on edge.

"Sounds like the I.R.A. fighting it out," commented Mr. Jackson as he sat drinking tea in the kitchen at two o'clock in the morning.

"How do you know?" said Sadie. "Could be anybody."

"I don't know what we're all doing sitting here," said Mrs. Jackson. She scratched her scalp between the rollers and yawned. "It's not as if we haven't heard the sound of guns before. It's funny how you get used to the murders after a bit."

"You can get used to anything," said Tommy. "You have to live."

Sadie looked at the clock. She ought to go to bed and get a few hours sleep. She planned to leave the house before seven to go and meet Kevin but now she was afraid that she might sleep in and he would be sitting waiting for her in a field twenty miles outside Belfast, watching the road, thinking she was never coming. But he would wait, she knew that.

"What are you smiling about?" asked her mother. "Can't see anything very funny about shooting matches myself."

"I was thinking of something else." Sadie stood up. "I'm off to bed. Oh, and by the way, I'll be going out early in the morning so don't worry if I'm gone when you get up."

"And where are you off to?"

"I'm spending the day with the Hendersons."

"I don't know why you don't move out there while you're at it."

Sadie left them drinking more cups of tea and went up to bed. She lay listening to the noises and gradually drifted into sleep.

It was light when she woke. It was past seven. She leapt out of bed and pulled on some clothes. As she was brushing her hair she heard a car come down the road slowly and stop outside. Pulling back the curtain she saw that it was the Hendersons' car. Mike Henderson got out and knocked on their door.

"Who in the name is that at this hour of the morning?" She heard her father's voice as she raced down the stairs. Her parents always slept with the door of their bedroom open.

She opened the front door. She looked at Mike's face and then said, "What's wrong?"

"Can I come in?"

She nodded. He stepped into the narrow hallway.

"Who is it, Sadie?" called her mother.

"It's Mr. Henderson."

"Mr. Henderson?" The bed springs creaked, followed by muttering overhead.

Sadie took Mike into the kitchen, closed the door.

"Tell me quickly," she said. "They'll be down in a minute to see what's going on."

"Sadie—" Mike paused; he put his hands on her shoulders. "I've got bad news for you."

"I can see that." Her eyes widened. She felt that she had lived through this moment before. "Has something happened to Mr. Blake?"

"Yes."

Footsteps above now.

"What is it? Is he dead?"

Mike nodded.

"He can't be dead," Sadie cried. "I saw him yesterday."

"Someone threw a petrol bomb into his house last night. The place went up in minutes and he didn't get out."

"Oh no!" Sadie stared at Mike. It was impossible to believe. It was a mistake, a dream, a nightmare.

"Swine!" said Mike bitterly, anger blazing in his eyes. "He never hurt anyone in his life."

Sadie sat down at the table. "Is it true?" she asked. Now she was beginning to know that it was. The knowledge was seeping through to her brain.

Mike sat down beside her. "I'm afraid it's true," he said, quiet now.

Sadie was weeping with her head on the table and Mike's arms round her shoulders when Mrs. Jackson came in.

"What's going on?"

"Sadie's had a shock, Mrs. Jackson."

Sadie lifted her head. "Mr. Blake's been killed, Ma."

"Killed?" Mrs. Jackson put her hand to her throat.

"His house was bombed last night."

Mr. Jackson came in with his shirt hanging over his trousers, followed by Tommy in his pyjamas.

"Sadie's Mr. Blake's been murdered," said Mrs. Jackson to them.

"It's my fault," cried Sadie. "It's my fault."

"Don't be silly, Sadie," said Mike. "You mustn't say that."

"It's true, it's true!"

Mr. Jackson shook his head. "What's it all about? How is it your fault, Sadie?"

"It isn't, Mr. Jackson," said Mike. "She's had a shock. She doesn't know what she's saying."

"I think I'd better make a cup of tea." Mrs. Jackson lifted

the kettle. "Jim, get her a glass of brandy from the front room."

Mr. Jackson, moving in a state of bewilderment, went to fetch the brandy. Tommy sat down on the other side of his sister. The gas flame hissed under the kettle.

"I don't know what the world's coming to," said Mr. Jackson. "You never know who'll be next."

Sadie took the glass from her father and drank. She felt sick. She wanted to vomit.

"Take another sip," said Mike. "It'll settle your stomach."

"I think you'd better tell us what happened," said Mr. Jackson.

Mike told them what he knew, which was little. No one had seen the bomb being thrown. No one had noticed any strangers in the district. It was not an area accustomed to bombing. There had never been any trouble there before. Sadie quietened. She dried her tears, drank her sweet tea, leaning on the table for support. She felt weak right to the centre of her body.

Then she remembered Kevin who would have set out already for their meeting place, not knowing what had happened. She looked at Mike. "If you're going now I'll come with you."

He nodded, knowing by the expression in her eyes that she was thinking of Kevin.

"There's no call for you to go, Sadie," said her father.

"I want to go."

"I want you to stay in."

"He's right," said her mother. "There's nothing for you to do anyway."

"I must go. *I must*."

"Let her go," said Tommy. "She'll come to no harm."

"I'll look after her," said Mike.

Mrs. Jackson sighed. "Oh, all right."

Kevin was there, at the spot they had arranged, lying on a grassy bank on his back, with the sun on his face. He sat up when he heard the car.

"Well, this is a surprise," he said, smiling at Mike. Mike and

152

Sadie sat down beside him, one on either side. Kevin frowned. "Is there anything up?" he asked.

"I'm afraid so," said Mike.

It was a big funeral. Mr. Blake had been well known and liked in the neighbourhood. Sadie sat with Moira in her house watching the procession pass down the street. She saw Kevin's head bent down, his face bleak below the dark fall of hair. Sadie gulped, covering her mouth with her hands.

"Come on, honey," said Moira. "Have this cup of coffee."

Sadie took the cup and drank, like an obedient child. In the last few days she had drunk more cups of tea and coffee than she would have thought possible. It was something to do. She had never known days could be so long. She went to bed exhausted at night and wept in her pillow and wakened exhausted in the morning to think at once of Mr. Blake.

"It doesn't seem possible," she said.

Moira sank into an armchair. She, too, looked tired and drawn. The children were staying with her mother in the country who was worried in case the bomb-thrower might choose the Hendersons as his next target. "You never know, Moira," her mother had said. "After all, you're Catholic and Mike's Protestant. I told you you'd have trouble some day. It's not that I'm not fond of Mike, you know that I am, but it would have been easier if he'd been Catholic."

Mike had said his mother-in-law was talking rubbish, that there was no chance of them getting a bomb through the window but Moira had said that it might be as well to have the children out of the way until the funeral was over, and the fresh country air would do them good. She might even go down and spend a week with them herself afterwards. "Why don't you go and live there?" Mike had flung back at her and they had almost had a row. She knew that he himself was anxious about the whole situation in the city.

"We ought to be used to things like this," said Moira. "But when it happens to a friend you feel bewildered at the idea of people wanting to kill."

After the funeral service Mike and Kevin came back. Mike bent over Moira to kiss her and asked, "You all right?" She nodded.

Kevin sat down beside Sadie on the settee. She slipped her hand into his. It was ice cold. "Hello," he said, trying to smile at her.

"Hello," she said softly.

"I think I need a little whisky to warm me up." Mike opened the sideboard door. "What about you, Kevin? Do you good."

"Just a little."

Mike raised his glass to Kevin's. "Well," he said, "here's to the memory of Mr. Blake. We won't forget him."

"We certainly won't," said Kevin. "And if I ever get my hands on the louts that did it I'll kill them!" His eyes flashed and colour spread across his cheeks.

"You wouldn't want to, would you, Kevin?" said Mike.

Kevin subsided. He shook his head. "No, I wouldn't want to ... But there's times when I feel such rage inside me ..."

"I know," said Mike quietly. "I feel rage too. But I don't want their blood on my hands."

Kevin looked down at the hand that held Sadie's and tightened his hold on hers. "No, I wouldn't want their blood on me either," he said. "Will you come for a walk with me, Sadie?"

They walked on Cave Hill, above the city.

"I've been thinking," he began.

"Yes?"

He turned and looked into her face and said quickly, "Sadie, I've got to go away. I can't stay here any longer. I haven't a job and I'm sick of bombs and people getting killed! And now that this has happened with Mr. Blake ..." He paused, then continued, "It's not a case of running away, you mustn't think that. I just don't want any part of what's going on here. I don't like the way we've got to live. It's not living anyway. Not living the way I want it."

She did not speak for a moment. She stared down at Belfast Lough lying below, seeing it blur and then come sharply into focus again. She swallowed. "When will you go?" she asked.

"Next week."

Chapter Twenty

Brede finished cutting the sandwiches and laid them in a plastic lunch box. Her mother was pouring tea from the kettle into a thermos flask. Her face was hot and flushed. Her eyes were on the golden brown stream of liquid, watching carefully that not a drop would spill, but her mind was on something else. Her eldest son was going away.

She covered the stopper with greaseproof paper, pushed it in to the neck of the flask. She looked round at her husband. He sat at the table in his shirt-sleeves, reading the evening paper, scratching his head. He had tried to talk Kevin out of going away, but not very convincingly. He knew that Kevin could not wander the streets indefinitely without a job. Besides, the streets were no place to wander these days. And it was not the first time a family had seen one of its children cross the water to England to get work.

Kevin came into the kitchen wearing his suit. She had bought it for him two years back for church-going. He had broadened since then and now it pulled across his shoulders. His mother took a handkerchief from her overall pocket and blew her nose.

He put his hands on her shoulders. "Hey, come on now," he said. "It's not that bad. I'll be back to see you in no time at all. Anyway, I thought you'd be glad to be rid of me for a while."

"One less shirt to wash and iron," said Brede, trying to fall in with his banter.

"One less mouth to feed," said Kevin.

"And a big one at that," said Brede.

"I'll be sending you money too," said Kevin.

"You'll need to get a job first," said his father.

"I'm not worried about that. They're all waiting for me over there to land." Kevin patted his mother's shoulder and walked over to the mirror to straighten his tie. He hated wearing a tie and seldom did, but it would please his mother to see him departing in a suit and tie, neat and respectable, and a credit to her.

"Better not be thinking the streets of Liverpool are paved with gold," said Mr. McCoy. "I hear there's plenty out of work there too."

"Who said anything about Liverpool?" Kevin gave the tie a final twist. "I might go to London."

"London?" said Mrs. McCoy doubtfully, for the sound of that was worse than Liverpool which could be reached by only crossing over a stretch of water. "It's a big city."

"The bigger the better! There, how do I look?"

"The girls of London will fall about when they see you," said Brede.

"Aye, they'll likely think I'm a right looking eejit." He laughed, and so did Brede.

He glanced quickly at the red and cream kitchen clock on the dresser. His mother's eyes swivelled to it too.

"I'll have to be off, Ma."

She nodded. She set the plastic box of sandwiches and flask on the table. "Have you room for them in your case?"

"Thanks, Ma." He lifted his case on to the table, opened it and put in the food. His mother fussed over the flask, insisting on wrapping it in a napkin in case the tea would leak out over his clothes.

"Your Uncle Albert would have run you to the boat," said Mr. McCoy.

"I didn't want any fuss."

"It doesn't seem right to be going away without one of your family to see you off," said Mrs. McCoy.

"Would you not like me to come with you, Kevin?" asked Brede.

"I'd just as soon go alone."

"O.K."

"You could walk down the street with me though."

She reached for her coat that hung on the back of the door. Mr. McCoy stood up. He cleared his throat.

"You'll write?" he said.

"As soon as I'm settled."

"Watch the company you keep, and don't do anything rash." Mr. McCoy put his hand in his pocket. "Here's an extra fiver. You might need it." When Kevin protested, he pushed the note into his hand. "Go on, take it. It's not often you get the chance of a fiver from me. One of these days I'll maybe be in need of one myself and then I'll come to you."

"I'll keep you in comfort in your old age, Da."

"Aye, that'd be right!" Mr. McCoy held out his hand to Kevin. "Good luck, son."

"Thanks, Da." Kevin took his father's hand.

"Brede," said Mrs. McCoy, "call the children and tell them Kevin's leaving."

"Kevin's leaving." The call went down the street; the children came running.

Kevin kissed his mother in the hall. She would cry after he had gone but her eyes were dry now. She told him to see that he got enough food to eat and to make sure that he found digs with a comfortable bed and she hoped if possible he would find a place in a good Catholic family. "God look to you, Kevin," she said and went back into the kitchen and closed the door.

A crowd of children were jumping up and down on the pavement.

"It's lucky you are going away on a boat," said Gerald.

"Don't I know it?" said Kevin.

Brede waited for him a few yards further down the street. She stood with her hands bunched into the pockets of her coat.

"Good-bye then, kids! Good-bye, Da."

"Good-bye, Kevin."

They called and waved until he was half-way down the street. He walked backwards waving his arm. And then he turned to Brede and said, "Let's go quickly now."

Mrs. Rafferty was standing on the opposite pavement. "Is that you for off then, Kevin? Off to make your fortune, eh?"

"You never know, do you, Mrs. Rafferty?" Brede called back.

When they rounded the corner, Kevin stopped. He put down the case. "You don't need to come any further, Brede. I want to go the rest of the way myself. You don't mind?"

"Of course not." She gave him a little smile. "Well, Kevin, I'll miss you."

"I'll miss you too. You'll write and tell me how everybody is? And if there's anything wrong you must let me know. Promise?"

She promised. She kissed him quickly on the cheek and then ran back round the corner, out of sight.

He picked up the suitcase and set off again. Ahead, at the entrance to the scrapyard, he saw Kate Kelly. She was leaning against the gate post watching him. As he came nearer she straightened up and came towards him.

"Can I speak to you, Kevin?"

"I've nothing to say to you."

"I just wanted to say I was sorry. I must have made a mistake about that box." She was walking beside him now in the direction of the bus stop. He lengthened his stride.

"You don't expect me to believe that!"

"Well, to be honest ... Brian Rafferty made me. I wouldn't have told the lie otherwise."

"Made you?" As he spoke he realised that he was not interested in what she had to say. It was all of it behind him now, Kate and Brian Rafferty and the beatings up and the bombs. He was heading out for something new. For the first time since deciding to go away he felt excitement stir inside him.

He saw a bus coming along the main road. "Good-bye, Kate," he said, and ran to meet it.

The ships' funnels loomed up behind the sheds. He sniffed in the exciting smell of the docks, a mixture of sea and oil and sacks. He walked, swinging his case, enjoying the bustle and movement around him.

Standing beside the Liverpool shed was Sadie. He ran the last few yards to reach her.

"So you managed to come and see me off?"

"Did you think I wouldn't?"

"No."

"Anyway, I haven't come to see you off. I'm coming with you." He was looking at her in amazement. She added anxiously, "You don't mind, do you?"

"Mind?" He put down his suitcase and lifted her up and whirled her round till she was breathless with laughter. "That's the best news I've had in months. But where's your luggage?"

"I couldn't walk out of the house with a case, could I now? You'll have to take me as I stand. But I've bought my ticket."

She took the piece of paper from her pocket and held it out.

"Come on then," said Kevin. "What are we waiting for?"

"Nothing," said Sadie. "Nothing at all."

He took her hand and together they walked across the shed to the white, waiting ship.

ALSO IN

**HEINEMANN
NEW WINDMILLS**

General Editors: Anne and Ian Serraillier

Chinua Achebe Things Fall Apart
Vivien Alcock The Cuckoo Sister; The Monster Garden; The Trial of Anna Cotman
Michael Anthony Green Days by the River
Bernard Ashley High Pavement Blues; Running Scared
J G Ballard Empire of the Sun
Stan Barstow Joby
Nina Bawden On the Run; The Witch's Daughter; A Handful of Thieves; Carrie's War; The Robbers; Devil by the Sea; Kept in the Dark; The Finding; Keeping Henry
Judy Blume It's Not the End of the World; Tiger Eyes
E R Braithwaite To Sir, With Love
F Hodgson Burnett The Secret Garden
Ray Bradbury The Golden Apples of the Sun
Betsy Byars The Midnight Fox
Victor Canning The Runaways; Flight of the Grey Goose
John Christopher The Guardians; Empty World
Gary Crew The Inner Circle
Jane Leslie Conly Racso and the Rats of NIMH
Roald Dahl Danny, The Champion of the World; The Wonderful Story of Henry Sugar; George's Marvellous Medicine; The BFG; The Witches; Boy; Going Solo; Charlie and the Chocolate Factory
Andrew Davies Conrad's War
Anita Desai The Village by the Sea
Peter Dickinson The Gift; Annerton Pit; Healer
Berlie Doherty Granny was a Buffer Girl
Gerald Durrell My Family and Other Animals
J M Falkner Moonfleet
Anne Fine The Granny Project
F Scott Fitzgerald The Great Gatsby
Anne Frank The Diary of Anne Frank
Leon Garfield Six Apprentices
Graham Greene The Third Man and The Fallen Idol; The Power and the Glory; Brighton Rock

Marilyn Halvorson Cowboys Don't Cry
Thomas Hardy The Withered Arm and Other Wessex Tales
Rosemary Harris Zed
L P Hartley The Go-Between
Esther Hautzig The Endless Steppe
Ernest Hemingway The Old Man and the Sea; A Farewell to Arms
Nat Hentoff Does this School have Capital Punishment?
Nigel Hinton Getting Free; Buddy; Buddy's Song
Minfong Ho Rice Without Rain
Janni Howker Badger on the Barge; Isaac Campion
Monica Hughes Ring-Rise, Ring-Set
Shirley Hughes Here Comes Charlie Moon
Kristin Hunter Soul Brothers and Sister Lou
Barbara Ireson (Editor) In a Class of Their Own
Jennifer Johnston Shadows on Our Skin
Toeckey Jones Go Well, Stay Well
James Joyce A Portrait of the Artist as a Young Man
Geraldine Kaye Comfort Herself; A Breath of Fresh Air
Clive King Me and My Million
Dick King-Smith The Sheep-Pig
Daniel Keyes Flowers for Algernon
Elizabeth Laird Red Sky In the Morning
D H Lawrence The Fox and The Virgin and the Gypsy; Selected Tales
Harper Lee To Kill a Mockingbird
Laurie Lee As I Walked Out One Midsummer Morning
Julius Lester Basketball Game
Ursula Le Guin A Wizard of Earthsea
C Day Lewis The Otterbury Incident
David Line Run for Your Life; Screaming High
Joan Lingard Across the Barricades; Into Exile; The Clearance; The File on Fraulein Berg
Penelope Lively The Ghost of Thomas Kempe
Jack London The Call of the Wild; White Fang
Lois Lowry The Road Ahead; The Woods at the End of Autumn Street
Bernard Mac Laverty Cal; The Best of Bernard Mac Laverty
Margaret Mahy The Haunting; The Catalogue of The Universe
Jan Mark Thunder and Lightning; Under the Autumn Garden

How many have you read?